CROSSING THE LINE

Crossing the Line is currently on:
UK Literacy Association Book Awards 2023 (longlist)
Southern Schools Book Award 2023 (shortlist)
Warwickshire Teen Book Awards 2023 (longlist)
YLG South East Yoto Carnegie Medal for Writing 2023
(shortlist for regional nomination)
Bristol Teen Book Awards 2023 (shortlist)

'A **gripping** verse novel packed with voice and emotion.' *Irish Independent*

'Addictive reading'. *School Reading List*

'Pulls no punches.' *Books for Keeps*

'A gripping read that packs a real punch. **Compelling, gutsy and important**, *Crossing the Line* is a stunning debut.' Lucy Cuthew, author of *Blood Moon*

'Offers real insight into how children are groomed and coerced by adult criminals' Claire Alldis National Disrupting Exploit

'A verse novel for our times.' Finbar Hawkins, author of *Stone*

'This is a book that needs to be in every school and library.' Kevin Cobane, member of the Empathy Lab judging panel

'This is an outstanding and important novel that should be widely read by parents and teachers as well as by the young people who will find it gripping, **relatable, authentic and unputdownable**.' LoveReading4Kids

'A book which will appeal to teens who know about gang culture and is a window into that lifestyle for those who don't.' Read for Good

'A fantastic YA verse novel that is **brutally honest**.' Book Riot

'[Draws] the reader in through every line . . . This captivating verse novel speaks of the risks young people face in becoming involved in gangs and offers a plethora of advice.' *Children's Books Ireland*

'A tough read at times, but highly recommended.' *Paper Lantern Journal*

'Eye-opening, **compelling**, and with characters I deeply care about. This is a book that **will make a real difference**.' Zana Fraillon, author of *Way of Dog*

'*Crossing the Line* is the first book I have ever finished other than *We're Going on a Bear Hunt* and *Dinosaurs Love Underpants*.' Mason, Year 8

CROSSING
THE
LINE

TIA FISHER

HOT
KEY
BOOKS

First published in Great Britain in 2023 by
HOT KEY BOOKS
4th Floor, Victoria House, Bloomsbury Square, London WC1B 4DA
Owned by Bonnier Books, Sveavägen 56, Stockholm, Sweden
bonnierbooks.co.uk/HotKeyBooks

A CIP catalogue record for this book is available from the British Library.

ISBN: 978-1-4714-1304-9
Also available as an ebook and in audio

3

Additional typesetting by Envy Design Ltd
Printed and bound in Great Britain by Clays Ltd, Elcograf S.p.A.

Hot Key Books is an imprint of Bonnier Books UK
bonnierbooks.co.uk

To the real Erik – and all the others like him.
One day you will feel safe again.

A question for you:

do you feel *safe*?

Safe.

Like opening your front door
    & just walking out,
like not sniffing the air for danger,
    checking
        left-right left-right
        left-right left-right,
cautious as a little kid
    crossing the road.

Safe.

Like the map of your city
    isn't riddled with hOles
    of black scorched
    no-go postcodes
where your life's
    worth less than paper.

Safe.

Like waving Mum goodbye
    & not thinking
    the next time she sees you
you might be on a slab.

You know.
That kind of safe.

It's been so long

since I wasn't afraid;
it's been years
    since I wasn't always looking
    over my shoulder.

I'm so *tired.*

I reckon the last time I felt
   really
      really
         really
           safe

was the first day of . . .

HOLLAND ROAD SECONDARY

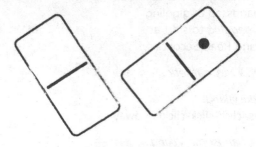

Click!

Picture this.

I'm standing on our doorstep
    in a brand-new too-big blazer,
    with a nervous too-wide smile.

I'm eleven.
Happy.
Got no idea of what's about to
    hit me.

I'm squinting into the September sun,
    at Dad's enormous
    grin of pride.

Dad's face . . .

It rips my heart
    when I think of it now.

I'm hopping from
    foot to shiny new-shoed foot,
    embarrassed & giggling
but still *gagging* to start at
    Holland Road Secondary.

Honestly, I was *pathetic.*

Min kjekke viking,
Dad says, click-click-clicking away.

I was his *handsome Viking.*
Yuck.

Is that Swedish? Close. Norwegian.
I always thought it sounded
    such a stupid language.
Still do.

Never learned,
  & it's too late now.

For goodness sake, Andreas!
That's Mum,
grabbing the camera
  from Dad's hands.
You'll make Erik late!

I hate the stupid way
  my parents spelled my name.

I hate a lot of things these days.

Why didn't anybody warn me?

I'll never understand.

No one said a word,
  right through primary,
No one even mentioned it.
It just wasn't a *thing*.

How could they have let me
  simply *stroll*
  into secondary school,
holding my head up
  like I had nothing to hide,
  nothing to be ashamed of?

That first morning,

Ravi & me
    stream out of assembly
& slip into a torrent of children
    tumbling past.

Ravi? He's my best mate from primary.
He's a bit different too –
    but in a different way.

We hold on to each other
    to keep afloat:
a couple of Year Seven
    insignificant twiglets
    swept into an adolescent flood.

Somehow, we make it.

Somehow, we beach ourselves
    the right way up,
    outside the right room,
    at the right time,
& queue up
    with the rest of 7M.

I don't know it yet, but
    I'm about to get rinsed,
    big time.

Oy!

Someone bumps me
    deliberately hard & I cannon into Ravi.

Whoops!
    the someone says,
    laughing in my face.

He's maybe Year Nine?
Skinny, tall,
    a flop of black hair,
    a wispy moustache.

The boy beside him stops too.
He's shorter & square-shaped,
    his pitted skin
    rough as an avocado.

Avocado Face looks me
    up & down
& I guess what he sees
    amuses him.

Slap the ginger!
    he shouts to his mate

& I don't even get time to
    du—
before
I get a ringer
    round my head.

                        OW!
                What was that for?

My attackers swagger off, cracking up
    like I'm the funniest thing
    they've seen in years.

Wanker!

It's a mutter under my breath
but Avocado Face
    must have supersonic hearing.

His head whips round.
WHAT. DID. YOU. SAY?
A broken voice that rumbles
    with the menace
    of thunder.

The chattering line hushes.
Ravi puts his hand on my arm.
Leave it! he whispers,
& I know I should,
    but I can't.

I'm just not made that way.

        You heard me! I say,
        wishing *fear* wasn't
        strangling my words
        to a squeak.

You heard me!
Tall boy bleats.

Don't we talk all nice?
Avocado Face moves
    back towards me.
*You say that again, Ginger,
    & I'll bang your face!*

Ravi steps away – fast.
Who can blame him?
I'm in for a beating.

Seems like bad decisions

stack like dominoes.
When one topples, they all go.
    Clackety-
        clackety-
            clackety-
                clackety-
                    clackety-
                        clackety-
                            clackety-
                              CLACK,
                              all the way down.

Looking back,
maybe this was
    the first domino to topple?

The misstep
    that kicked off
    the run.

I think this must be a record!

The head teacher's lips
    crinkle tight
like the drawstring of a shoe bag.
He narrows his eyes.

Shouts drift up
    from the field
    & bounce off the window.

It's break time already.
I've spent the whole first period
sitting like an idiot
outside Mr Nelson's office.

It's the first time
    ANYONE has EVER
been sent to see me
    for fighting
    on their very first day!
he says.

I bet it isn't.

Outside, a group of
    boys weave a tight knot
    in the far corner of the field.
Smoke curls a wispy signal.

Actually –
the head teacher
    checks his watch
        for effect –
in their very first hour.

I run my tongue around my
mashed-up mouth
but Mr Nelson doesn't invite me
to open it
in self-defence.

When the head teacher finally

lets me go,
I spend ages looking for
    the geography room
where I'm supposed to have
    period three.

All the corridors
    look the same,
ghost-town empty of
    their teenage traffic.

When I finally
    locate Room G3,
I tap on the door
    as quietly as I can.

A tall, bearded teacher
    is standing by the board.
He nods curtly at me
    to enter.

He makes me sit alone
    on a table at the front
    while he talks about
        archipelagos.

I'm marooned
    on this island
    in a sea full of stares.

I can feel my ears burning,
    red as my hair.

Having red hair is *not* OK!

We should've
   dyed it,
      shaved it,
         waxed or wigged it –
made up some excuse,
said I was having chemo or something.

No one should've
   allowed me to believe
   there was nothing
   wrong with me.

Why didn't someone tell me
   having red hair is not okay?

My best friend looks

embarrassed
   as we file into lunch.

Sorry, he says,
picking up a small plastic tray
   spattered with
   someone else's gravy.
Sorry I didn't help back there.

               S'okay, I say, fishing out my fob
               & wondering what I'm supposed
                    to do with it.
                  You're not exactly
                   a fighter . . .

How about, says Ravi,
pointing to the veggie option
& smiling at the dinner lady,
next time
    you keep your big gob shut
        instead?

Erik, there was actual *blood*!

I should have known
    Mum'd get a call:
as soon as I walk in
    she's on at me –

She's so shocked
she doesn't even ask
    about my day.

                        But, Mum . . .
                        I start –
            but she won't let me finish.

                    I want to say
            I can still taste my fear,
        the push of his arm pressed
                    across my neck,
    my heartbeat thud-thudding in my ears.

                    Pinned to the wall
            by painful rabbit punches,
                I couldn't breathe,
                I couldn't *breathe* –

                Of course I bit him.
                It was self-defence.

I'm called

Erik the Viking, of course,
but mostly it's

Oy! Gingernut!
           Copper-knob!
     Hey, ging-ga!

Yeah, you! Fanta-pants Posh Boy.

   Shut up, copper-bollox!

Carrot-top!   *It's GINGER NINJA!*

*Such a beautiful shade of auburn:
like a maple leaf in autumn,*
     Mum says.

She has absolutely
     no idea.

At the back

             of every
          form room, the
       lockers are like a wall
       of upright coffins: such a
          dumb idea because they're
                      just tall enough for
                      a Year Seven boy to
                      be squashed into, but
                         only if he bends both
                            his knees a bit, just a tiny
                               (agonising) five degrees
                                or so. They are in fact
                               so thin that a boy my
                            size   can only just
                                 expand his ribs
                               enough to suck
                            thin sips of air
                         & maybe it's
                      a design fault
                   they should
                   really have
                   considered:
                      that lockers
                         are only *un*
                            locked from
                               the outside:
                               & then only
                            if somebody cares
                         you're still there.

I'm a target.

At school I can't hide:
I stand out
    like a **bullseye**.

At least
    in lockdown
I can make myself

    invisible.

It's okay, really –

you don't have to
    feel sorry for me
    about this.

It's all such a
    long time ago

& there's so much else
    to be sorry for
    now.

LOCKDOWN

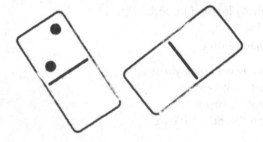

Do I remember

much about
   the first lockdown?

Of course I do.

You think I could forget it?
Don't be stupid.

I'm twelve years old
& my dad dies.

In lockdown, lessons

are mostly learned in bed:
   camera off,
   pyjamas on.

In biology we study viruses
   that look like
   depth charges
   from World War Two.

In history we do
   development of vaccines
& draw comparisons
   with Spanish flu.

Our Year Eight form teacher,
(who teaches economics
   to the sixth form),
says something
   darkly about *Malthus*
   that I still don't
   understand.

In citizenship, we debate the
    pros & suɔɔ of
    euthanasia –

at least the others do.

I make an early exit.

This is the year

loads of kids
    lose their grandparents,

but no one else at school
    was careless enough
    to lose their actual *dad.*

So you think

what happened to me
    has to do with
    what happened then?

Well, like, *duh.*

Yeah, maybe it
    would have helped
    to talk to somebody
    at the time –

but we were in lockdown,
    remember, &
I had to be strong for Mum –

I'd promised Dad.

Not gonna lie,

I'm scared to open up
    the box marked 'Dad'.

I still don't want to
    think about
    when my dad –
    when he –
    when he –

Hang on.

I'll be all right in a minute.

A day passes

without Dad.

The first Monday without him.

Then another.

The Mondays roll past
    like waves,
        knocking me off my feet
            until it's spring.

Even without Dad,
    flowers bloom.
The grass still grows.

But no one mows the lawn:

it's like we're waiting
    for him to
    come back.

Mum cries for months.

She says she feels so alone.

She says she feels like
    the last polar bear

                    adrift
                    on a tiny
                    shrinking
                    chunk of
                    ice.

                        What about me?
                        Aren't I enough?
                        I want to ask her.

                            But I don't.

My mum

pretty much raised herself
    in a care home.

My dad's folks
    disowned him
    when he married her.

We knew all about
    being abandoned
    already:

we didn't need
    another lesson.

It feels like we're waiting

for him to return
    forever.

We wait

      & wait

           & wait

until
    one day

my mum just
    gives up
    waiting.

JONNY

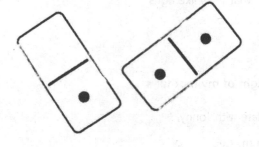

My dad hadn't even

been dead
    twelve months

before Mum goes on a date
    with some random bloke
    she met online.

I try to tell her
    that a year
    isn't nearly long enough.

She says
    I've got no idea
    how long a year can be.

Then we don't speak
    for what feels like ages.

The night of my mother's

third date with Jonny,

I lie on my bed
    on sandpaper sheets,
watching my phone
    blink the day into touch.

When she
      finally
          creeps in

it's the traitorous little sounds,
    the squeaks of stifled laughter,
    the
        double creak
                of stairs . . .

She's not sober.

She's not alone.

Jonny starts

staying over
    almost every night

& I start
    staying in my room,
    only coming out for food
    like a badger.

Jonny's cuckoo stink
    hangs around in the mornings.

That knock-off pong
    trails him out of the bathroom
    & down the stairs to breakfast,

where
    it rises like steam
    curling over the teacups.

Dad's favourite jumper

is sealed
    like evidence
    in an M&S bag
    at the bottom
    of my wardrobe.

It's only been
    fourteen months,
    but his smell
    is already
    beginning to fade.

I have to breathe in
    more deeply
    each time.

Why don't I give Jonny a key?

Mum asks,

except it's not really a question.

So now Jonny swaggers
    into the house –
    my house –
without even knocking.

Hello? Anyone home?
He whistles for her
    like he's calling
    a dog.

It makes me squirm
    as she comes trotting
    lipsticked down the stairs,

all done up like a
    welcome doormat.

I usually scoff my tea down

double quick
so I can escape
    from the sight of that man
sitting in Dad's place
    at the table.

                One day I'm legging it away,
            mouth still full of burger & fries,

when Jonny calls, *Hang on, Erik!*

             & I halt one-footed in the hall.

We've got a birthday surprise!
    he says.
Your mum & me.
How about coming to
    the re-opening of Alton Towers?

You two can
    get to know each other!
Mum chips in.

Jonny smiles his creepy smile
& I can't think of anyone
    I want to know
        less.

But then Mum says
Please, Erik?

                                          & I think,
                              Alton Towers?
            & moonwalk back into the room.
                       You've got tickets?

(Well, everybody's got their price.)

Relief,

like a damp flannel,

wipes the tension
    off my mother's face.

We used to go to Alton Towers

every single year.

We'd queue up for the scary rides,
my mum, my dad & me.

The *faster,*
                 the *higher,*
           the bigger,
the better.

But Mum says
    she'd rather disembowel herself
    than loop the loop today,

& actually she does
    go kinda green to prove it.

So in the end it's just Jonny & me.

Me & my Nemesis
    locked together
    for the ride.

Even having Jonny by my side

doesn't stop the thrill
as our carriage tilts, c-r-a-n-k-i-n-g
a crazy angle to the sky.

Normal life drops away.
I can see for miles & miles across the
    tangle of metal & treetops.

                      Any moment now
                        I'll lose control.
                            I love it.

The best bit is the wait until you start the
    delicious *tilting* over the edge

that breathless

       . . . pause . . .

              before the d
                       r
                       o
                       p.

Those seconds when it feels
   like life
   could change
   completely.

& it does.

Immediately.

Jonny digs me
   with his elbow

& totally messes up
   the rest
   of my life.

GUESS WHAT?
   he screams,
   over the screaming
   around us.

YOUR MOTHER'S PREGNANT!

YOU'RE GOING TO BE
A BIG BROTHER!

WHAT D'YOU THINK OF
   THAT, THEN?

What I *think*
sprays out of my mouth
in a messy spiral
as we roll over & over & over & over & over & over

& shock
punches my lunch
back up.

When I see Jonny touch her

I hate him I hate him I hate him
I hate him I hate him I hate him
I hate him I hate him I hate him
I hate him I hate him I hate him
I hate him I hate him I hate him
I hate him I hate him I hate him
I hate him I hate him I hate him
I hate him I hate him I hate him
I hate him I hate him I hate him
I hate him I hate him I hate him
I hate him I hate him I hate him
I hate him I hate him I hate him
I hate him I hate him I hate him
I hate him I hate him I hate him
I hate him I hate him I hate him
I hate him I hate him I hate him
I hate him I hate him I hate him
I hate him I hate him I hate him
I hate him I hate him I hate him
I hate him I hate him I hate him
I hate him I hate him I hate him
I hate him I hate him I hate him
I hate him I hate him I hate him
I hate him I hate him I hate him
I hate him I hate him I hate him
I hate him I hate him I hate him
I hate him I hate him I hate him
I hate him I hate him I hate him
I hate him I hate him I hate him
I hate him I hate him I hate him
I hate him I hate him I hate him
I hate him I hate him I hate him

& I hate her too.

I don't even know

exactly what Jonny does
    (apart from making babies,
    that is)

but whatever it is,
    he starts doing it
    for longer & longer
    each day.

In May he goes away
    for work
    for a whole two weeks.

Mum says he's got no choice,
    his firm's in trouble.

But since Covid,
    everyone's in trouble.
He's nothing special.

Mum used to run a
    cafe that doesn't even
    exist any more.

These days
    she looks so tired
    she couldn't run
        a bath.

Just before half-term

I'm walking home *sans* Ravi
cos I got detention
    for talking back
    in French.

(But not for talking back
    in *French,* which would be cool:
Ravi's teaching me some
    très bon words for *repartie.*)

It's raining &
    the wind is ripping
    sky-coloured   holes
    through the   black
            storm clouds.

Some summer
    this is.

I let myself in & the wind
    argues with the front door,
    banging it shut.

Dripping for a minute
    on the mat, I can hear
    the sound of crying somewhere.

                                    I shout, *Mum!*

But there's no reply,
    just that sobbing.

                                    Mum?

The kitchen door

bursts open
& Jonny pushes past me,
     shouting, *I CAN'T HANDLE THIS!*
     over his shoulder.

His tailwind buffets
     my face.

                                        Oh, I say.
                                   So. You're back.

He turns,
     one hand on the doorknob.
No,
     he says,
I'm not.

Slam.

35

Mum's collapsed

on the floor by the table,
    hugging her knees
    into her chest.

                Mum? Are you okay?

                Such a dumbass thing
             to say. As if she *looked*
                       okay.

I've got news,
    she says, wiping snot
    from her face.

It's twins,
    she says, & her eyes
    are a mess of mascara.

Looks like we hit the jackpot!
    she says, with a try
    at a smile.

I'm getting it now:
    that 'we'
    doesn't include
    Jonny.

& just like that

Jonny disappears,
  leaving only
  Mum's ballOOning belly
& a swelling debt
  to say he was ever here.

I would say
  we're better off
  without him,

but we're totally skint.

I'd rather just

skip over the next few months,
  if you don't mind.

No one's mum
  should be
  pregnant & abandoned.

That happens
  to teenagers. Not
  to teenagers' mums.

It's –
It's *embarrassing.*

It feels like

someone has
    unglued me.

Put the bits back
    all wrong.

I'm different now –

& I'm not sure
    I like myself
    this way.

THE TWINS

The twins arrived

too early, before I'd even opened

half my Advent windows –

Surprise!

I don't remember much
    about the birth –
I wasn't there,

thank God.

When I go to visit,

a freckled nurse
    swishes back the curtains:
pale grey drapes
the exact same shade
    as Mum's face.

She looks awful. Knackered.

Nearly as awful
    as Dad did when he –
    when he –

Look who's here!
    says the nurse.

But Mum doesn't *look*
    to see who's here:
she keeps her eyes
    on the newborn
    munching at her chest.

Hello, Erik, she says
    in a tired voice,
    thin as skimmed milk.

So I don't have to
    look there, at where
    the baby's slurping,
I check out the plastic box
    by her side.

Inside the aquarium,
    an identical screwed-up purple face
    is making a sound like a goat.

What d'you think of your
    Christmas presents, then?
asks Mum.

                    I shrug.
                What am I
          supposed to say?

I stay at Ravi's

while Mum bonds
    with her new babies
    on the ward.

Mrs Choudhri
    fusses, heats spiced milk,
    makes me so welcome
I don't want to leave.

Mr Choudhri
    asks Ravi
    about his day

in a way
    that somehow
    makes me
    sad.

Back home again

& our house
gets very crowded,
    very quickly,
like a lift when
    everyone piles in
    on the ground floor.

It definitely feels like we're
    over *max. persons*.

I'm squeezedout, literally –
    there's just no room for me
    any more.

I even have to
    give the twins my bedroom:

I've got Dad's old study
    in the attic
    with the screaming sound of
                newborns
                underneath.

It's late December.

The attic's freezing.

At least I can
    keep my hands warm
    on a real Christmas present:
my brand new (okay, secondhand)
    PlayStation.

Ravi asks me,

are my sisters cute?

Cute?
Is he *serious*?

Esme/Alice* wakes.
Esme/Alice* cries.
Esme/Alice* feeds, burps, poos herself
    then falls asleep.

Repeat,
repeat,
repeat.

I honestly can't tell
   one boring
   pain-in-the-butt
   twin sister
   from the other.

                                        * Delete as applicable.

At New Year

my best friend pops over.

I try to go round his instead,
   but he insists.
I haven't been to yours
   for ages.

                           Yeah. There's a reason for that.

Wow! he says,
   as he squeezes himself between
   the piles of washing,
                 the buggies
   & the bouncy chairs.
This place has changed.

                                        No kidding.

44

Turns out,

not only is Ravi
    like a dumpster stuffed
    to overspilling with
    the weirdest random stuff
    he's always trying to cram into my head,
    like the answers to:

What does 'etiolated' mean?
How many sides does a heptadecagon have?
How does guano differ from other bird droppings?
What's an event horizon?
What currency do they use in Denmark?

& not only can he
    sing the lyrics
    to *every. single. track*
    (not even joking)
    of his father's
    massive vinyl collection,

but he also knows
    an entirely inappropriate amount
    about babies.

When Alice (Esme?) starts bawling,
    he picks her up,
    his hand beneath her head,

& jiggles her a bit,
    whistling 'Baby Don't Cry'.

45

In my attic room,
    he confesses he just likes babies.
I've got lots of cousins. They're sweet.
Then he blushes.

So he should.

Erik!

Eriiiik!

ERIIIIKKKKKK!

I try to ignore her calls,
    louder & louder
        u
        p
two flights of stairs,
    t^{a}n$_g$li^{n}g in
    the banisters,

wedging themselves
    firmly between me
        &
    the numbers on the page.

Finally, I snap
    my textbook shut
    & stand up.

Baby work
    makes maths revision
    look like fun.

                              I'm COMING!!!

What is it now?

Bottles.

I lose count
    of how many bottles
    I scrub & sterilise & fill
to plug those
    gummy mouths.

Washing.

I drape rows & rows of babygrows
    on radiators,
    like lines of
    j^{a}g^{g}e^d teeth.

Rocking.

I rock my sisters

      ^{to} & fro
          fro & ^{to}
    ^{to} & fro
        fro & ^{to}

until I think
    my rocking arms
    are gonna drop.

I get it
    that it's tough for Mum,
but *she chose* to have the babies.

I didn't.

In the meantime

my homework's piling up
    like the snowdrifts
    on my
    sloping attic windows.

Please

can we stop
talking about
the babies now?

It does my head in.

Let's talk about
    how shit school was.

Please.

BROKE &
BROKEN

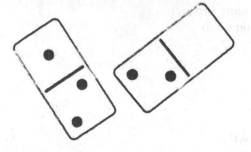

By week two of

the spring term
        of Year Nine
I'm so tired
I'm beaten like an egg.

I almost want
    Jonny to come back,
    just to do his share.

Halfway through
    English lit,
my desk becomes
    a whirlpool,
    a sticky black gravity hole
    that sucks me in
    over the event horizon.

I've just *gotta* lay
    my heavy head
    down on my arms . . .

Jeckyll turns into
Hyde turns into

sleep.

Wake up!

hisses Ravi, but
    before I can
    jerk my head off the desk

Mrs Raynor swishes down
  a roll of homework
  a centimetre
  from my nose.

That's the third time this term!
What's wrong with you, Erik?
  She points me towards
  the welfare office.

I don't tell the welfare officer
  about the endless chores,
  about the crying,
  about being fished out of sleep
  a dozen times a night.

Mum says,
  if anyone asks how we're doing
  I should always say, *FINE.*
We don't need any help.

When one sister stops,
  the other cranks it up, like
  human alarm clocks going off
  right under my bed.

You can go crazy
  from lack of sleep.
Ravi says it's an actual *torture.*

The welfare officer & I
  talk about mindfulness
& I promise not to stay up
  playing games.

How did it go? asks Ravi,
  as I slide back in beside him.

Fine, I say.

Next time

the welfare officer
    isn't so sympathetic.

No more mindfulness
    (thank God).

We talk about my grades,
    which are heading downhill
    as fast as a lorry with
    broken brakes.

We talk about how
    I had better smarten up
    my act, *or else*.

We talk about what a shame it is
    I'm letting my potential
    go to waste.

Or rather, the welfare officer does, because

                I'm too tired
                    to talk.

                I'm too tired
            even to paste on
            the right expression
      when he tells me to go:
the face that says, *I'm sorry.*

      I don't say, *Thank you, sir.*
        I say, *Yeah, whatever.*

So I get time out
    in the Blue Room
    too.

They 'remove' you to the Blue Room

when you've turned the air
    blue with swears,
when you've bashed an eye
    blue with bruises,
when you're feeling so blue
    you lash out.

That's why they call it
    the Blue Room.

Nah, not really.

They call it the Blue Room
    because the walls are blue.
Blue's supposed to be calming,
    but there's nothing calm
    about being in here.

The Blue Room's where the
    trouble kids come,
    the kids I try to keep away from.

Kids like Avocado Face
    & his *etiolated* mate,
kids who love to shout out
    Ginger! with a hard g
& bat me on the head
    as they go by.

In the Blue Room
    the teachers are more like
    prison guards.

You don't learn anything
    in the Blue Room –
    or at least, nothing
    a teacher would tell you.

To sign in to 'Remove'

you have to walk
    between the
    rows of desks

trying to ignore
    the catcalls
    & spitballs
    & flying rubbers

& it feels less like
    twenty steps

& more like a
    green mile.

After the Easter break

Year Nine gets a presentation:

we're getting a last bit of fun
before they prod us on to the
    treadmill of GCSEs.

At the end of term
    our year's going
    teambuilding:
sailing, climbing, building rafts;
a ton of fun.

But a week of watersports
    on the Isle of Wight
    costs more than
    seven nights in the Seychelles.

Ravi starts singing
　　some crappy song
　　about us all going
　　on a summer holiday –
but he's got that wrong.

We're not all going, are we?
Not at that price.

The list of things

I hate about being broke
　　is so long
　　you couldn't write it
　　on a single-ply
　　loo roll.

Just for starters, I hate not doing good stuff with my mates, I hate cheap baked beans, own-brand Coke, own-brand everything, walking everywhere, my big toe poking through my worn-out Vans, free school meals, Mum shouting three minutes! outside the shower & turning the thermostat down, no more Sky, going to the food bank, no treats, trips out or trainers, no steaks, no snacks, no skateboards

But most of all, I hate
　　the way Mum always says,
　　　It could be worse.
　　　At least we've all got each other.

Like that's not the problem.

Mum says she

doesn't know how
    we're going to manage.

Things were bad enough
    before the twins,
when we only had
    our own two
    mouths to feed.

One of us
    made some wrong choices,
    IMHO

& guess what?

It wasn't me.

Sometimes the twins

cry so hard
    there's no breath left &
    they go almost blue
    with rage.

I know it's wrong
    but I want to
    shock the air back
    into those lungs:

yell at them
    they've really got nothing
    to cry about –

seeing as
they don't know yet
    how *shit* life is.

Being skint sucks.

It sucks so hard.

As if free school dinners
    & second-hand uniform
    aren't enough humiliation,

I'm going to be
    the only Year Nine boy
    not on the end-of-year trip.

I can see it now:
    stuck at school, sat in
    the library for lessons,
    alone at break & lunch
    & snapping at the
    same
        stupid
                question –

Why ain't you with your mates, man?

When I tell Ravi

I'm not going
    to the Isle of Wight,
he really pisses me off
    by getting all sad

& not even singing
    a cheesy cheer-up tune.

Up until then,
    I was more or less
    keeping it
    together.

I'm on my own in SaverMart

cos Mum can't handle
    shopping with the babies,

& I spot the tall, thin, figure of
    Ravi's dad,
stooped over in the yogurt aisle,
squinting at the tiny writing on a pot.

He pats the pockets of the three-piece suit
    he always wears.
Ah, Erik! he says. *I forgot my glasses.*
Can you help me?

I read him the list of ingredients
    while Mr Choudhri keeps on looking, pulling out
    handkerchief, keys, calculator and pens
    like rabbits from a hat.

Later, when I empty my trolley,
    somehow there's a leaflet in the bottom
about the school's Hardship Fund:
    a pot of money to pay for trips
    that poor kids can't afford.

I get it then, that Ravi's kindly dad
    just set me up like a skittle,
saved me *and* my face.

It's Ravi's birthday next week.

Ravi & me
    & Jordan Ikes
    & a bunch of other
    9M dudes

hang out at break time,
planning Ravi's birthday treat.

Someone says, *Paintballing?*
& Ravi says, *Why not?*
    & checks it out
    on his phone.

Twenty quid a head.
Who's up for it? he asks.

Nine hands wave, *Yeah!*
    but there's one pair that only
    crack each other's knuckles
    like a feeble joke.

Ravi looks at his phone again.

Hang on – he says,
    did I say twenty?

Facepalm.
I'm shit at maths.

(He's not.)

It's twenty-two. All right?

I shake my head, but
    the nine other people
    who are now
    sharing the cost of me,
    nod, *Sure.*

& why not?

Two quid's
    small change
    to them.

Mum used to

be on my case all the time,
    checking my grades,

which were
    actually pretty high
    before the twins.

Sometimes she'd ask
    to see my homework.

We'd talk about school stuff.
    I'd wish she wouldn't.

This term
    does she even know
    how low my grades
    have sunk?
Does she even *care*?

At paintball,

Ravi & me get put on
    the same team.

Considering Ravi runs like a walrus
    & keeps singing crappy songs like
       'The Eton Rifles',
         'Rubber Bullets'
           & 'I Shot the Sheriff',
    we're surprisingly good.
(Must be all that practice
    on the PlayStation.)

The best bit's when
    this big bloke gets
    two bullets at the same time:
bright pink splodges
    like a blush on each
    butt cheek.

Then Ravi runs head first, *SMACK!*
    into a tree trunk.

His nose sprays like a hydrant:
    the inside of his visor runs scarlet
    like something out of *Alien*.

Even Ravi thinks it's funny (later).

At lunch
    we sit around on hay bales
    eating rubbish pizzas

& it's so good just to feel
    fourteen years old,
    having fun again.

The games are over.

All the teams
    pile into the shed to
    strip paint-peppered camos
    & compare our bruises.

But when I peel off my
    sweaty helmet
    there's a massive shout:

It's GINGER NINJA!

& I've suddenly stopped
    having fun.

Travis & Ben

(aka *Avocado Face* & *The Beanpole*)
    have evolved into
    Holland Road's notorious
    Year Eleven double act.

Double-trouble act.

You don't see one
    without the other:

Ben is Travis's
    right-hand man:
his shadow,
            his echo,^{echo}
                    the *splint that* props him up.

I wish

I was still holding
    my fake M16,
cos Travis is right behind me,
    his skinny shadow
    oil-slicked to his side.

I thought it was you!
    he says in triumph.
He turns to his mate.
Didn't I say
    it was that posh little
        Ginger Ninja?
        You know, Bitey Boy.

That's it.
I've had enough.
I don't have to
    take this any more:

two years have
    piled the inches on.
I'm looking down on Travis now.

I take a step in closer.
The name's Erik, I say.

& I'm not posh.

Take it easy, Erik!

Man, I was only joking!
The boy who tried
    to strangle me
    now holds his palms
    face up for peace.
Chill!

*Yeah, no need
    to be so sensitive!*
    says his skinny sidekick.

My friends have clocked this.
They're flanking me
    in case it all
    kicks off.

To my surprise, Travis
    sticks out a
    stubby hand.
No hard feelings, eh?

Almost as a reflex,
I shake.

64

TRAVIS & BEN

Year Nine have

MFL in second period,
    known to us as
    Mother-Fucking Languages
    (if you'll pardon my French).

Monsieur Lebron's a joke.
He's got a
    dumbass twirly moustache
    & is bald as an
    oeuf.

He's one of those teachers
    who banters with his
    favourites.

I used to be a favourite,
but I think I disappoint him
    maintenant.

This Tuesday we're doing
    physical descriptions
& I ask him what
    'baldy' is in French.
For a joke. A *joke*.

He gets narked &
    seriously takes the *pisse*
    out of my hair:
calls me a *poil de carotte*,
which is so completely
    out of order that
    I tell him to *casse-toi*
    & chuck a chair.

Sometimes,
    I get triggered.

So I'm removed

to the Blue Room
    again.

I push the scratched-up
    door & spot
my favourite comedy duo
    side by side
    as always.

The teacher at the desk
    asks my name
    & Travis looks up.

He fixes me with a frown,
fingers busy
    with his phone.

After half an hour

Travis chucks a paper ball
    over the partition. *Wot u in for?*

My scribbled reply
    gets scrunched up & *hopscotched* . . . .
    over the partitions
    like Chinese Whispers.

Turns out that
    chucking a chair at a teacher
& telling him to *eff off* in French
    kind of gives me
    Blue Room creds.

Respect!
Cool!
Good for you, Posh Boy!

For once
    my nickname
    doesn't feel
    like an insult.

From his booth,
Ben salutes me.

I feel like
    King of Remove.

The prison guard

in charge that day
has a marshmallow face
    on a body made of
        doughnut.

He hardly reacts
    to the blaring horn
    announcing lunchtime
    at Holland Road –
the kind of noise
    that would mean
        FIRE!
    anywhere else.

He just looks up
    & waves a weary hand.
We shoot out of our booths
    like we're jet-propelled.

Come to the Flo, says Travis,
    as we jostle
    through the door.
He nods to the main entrance.
Sixth-formers & Year Elevens
    are strolling through it
    cos they're allowed out.

I hesitate.
I've never cut school
    before, not ever.

But then, I never
    had anywhere else
    to go.

We'll get

lunch from the chippie,
    says Ben.

I don't want to tell him
I'm on free school meals,
I've got zero cash.

Stay with us.
Travis hustles me
    into the middle of
    a fat group of Year Elevens
    heading out the door.

Before I know it,
    I'm past the teachers
    & on the other side
    of the gate.

THE FLORENCE NIGHTINGALE
RECREATIONAL PLAYGROUND FOR CHILDREN

says the knackered old stone arch at the entrance. But
everyone just calls this place the *Flo*. A million years ago
they knocked down the kids' hospital, leaving the little
playground next to the big park & the arch sticking

up like an old	monument, like
Stonehenge	or something.
I used to	play here
as a kid	but now
it's all	rusty &
there's	guano
on the	swings,
broken	glass in
the grass,	& the only
fun skipping	game is kids
like Ben & Travis	skipping school.

When you're hungry

nothing beats chips:
    the sting of vinegar
& the warm weight
    leaking into your lap –
especially if they're free.

Even though I'd said
    I wasn't hungry,
when Ben walks out
    of the chip shop
he gives me a
    soggy paper parcel
& a silent nod.

I stuff them in
    as fast as I can,
sitting with my
    knees up to my chin
on a swing
    that squeals & shrieks.

Travis scrumples up
    his cardboard tray
& misses the bin.

He fishes in his pocket,
pulls out a pouch
& starts to roll, his
    ink-stained fingers deft & sure.

He tips, licks & sticks until –
like a wand –
    he taps three times

& *hey presto!*

it's done.

I was only in

Year Seven
    when I walked in on
    two sixth-formers
    in the second-floor loos.

Even then
    I knew it wasn't
    sherbet dipper
    they were dabbing
    on their gums.

They stared at me
    unhurriedly.

Piss off, one said.

So I peed at the speed
    of light

& left.

If they had exams

in knives & drugs & beatings,
    Holland Road Secondary
    would be right up
    in the tables.

Here, catch!

Pincering the spliff
    between fingers & thumb,
        Travis narrows his eyes
           & tosses it like a dart
    to Ben, who catches
& grins at me.
Smoke? he says.

I know

I said I wouldn't ever smoke,
I *know* I promised Dad,
I *know* I swore
    without my fingers
    crossed behind my back.

But Dad broke his promise too,
    didn't he?
He said he'd always be there.

So yeah, I feel bad,
    & yeah, I remember
    the promise I made.

But listen – he meant *cigarettes*, right?

Don't mind if I do,

I reply,
so cool,
so (in actual fact)
bricking it.

Just act natural,
I tell myself.

Naturally
I don't let on
I've never smoked before,
but my lungs feel
like I've lit a forest fire,
like I've crisped the
little air sacs,
so *naturally*
I choke & splutter.

Ben rolls his eyes
& takes the spliff from
my shaking fingers.

First time, yeah?
he says, & thumps me
on the back.
You'll get used to it.

Whatever

do we find to talk about,
Travis & Ben & Posh Boy?
I didn't think we'd have
that much in common but
there's more to life, apparently,
than 80s hits or Esme's colic or Minecraft –
or anything else I might talk about
with my straight-as-a-crate
weirdly odd mate,
Ravi.

RAVI

Hey, you missed the French test!

After school, Ravi
    scuttles up to join me
    two streets from my door.

I'm still feeling
    pretty . . . chilled.

He hands me a Creme Egg,
    warm from his damp palm.
Monsieur Lebron
    gave 'em out after class.
    Dunno why.
I snuck an extra one for you.

                                    Thanks, I say,
                            my mouth watering,
                        thumbnail already sliding
                                under the foil.

A Creme Egg has never
    tasted so sweet.
I wish that hairy-faced Frenchman
    could see me *mange* his chocolate
    cos it would really
    piss him off.

So, where d'you disappear to?
Ravi's bouncing along by my side.
Did they keep you
    in Remove all day?

                            Yeah . . . I say vaguely,
                        wiping my chocolatey hand
                                on his blazer.
                            Something like that . . .
                        & switch the subject over
                                to Minecraft.

When I get home that day,

my mother's hunched over
    a baby's bum &
    the kitchen stinks of poo.

The other sister's
    squalling on
    one note
    over & over & over:
        Wah! Wah! Wah!
        Wah! Wah! Wah!
        Wah! Wah! Wah!

Mum peers at me through
    a greasy curtain of hair,
    with eyes as
    bloodshot
    as Halloween sweets.
Would you get Alice, love?

The last of the warm fuzzies
    fades away.

I scoop Alice up

& her back
    is warm & wet.
    Urgh!
But then
    something happens . . .

She looks at me –
& the noises stop.

Alice crinkles up her eyes:
her mouth makes a sideways D.

My sister is *smiling*.
My sister is smiling at *me*.

Oh wow!

Her very first smile!
Specially for her big brother!
Mum hustles her phone
& Alice does one more for Facebook
    before falling asleep
    in my arms

as suddenly as
    an off switch.

Look!

Alice has eyelashes
    as delicate as
    cat hairs.

                              I reach out one
                              cautious finger
                          to brush her cheek,
                            but she doesn't
                              wake up.

It's so soft,
it's like touching
    candy floss.

Mum sees us
& for a moment
    she's looking at me
    just the way
    I'm looking at Alice.

This is nice, Mum says,
& pushes the plate
    towards me.
Have a shortbread.

The kitchen clock tick-tocks
    in a warm silence
    washed with the smell of milk.
I've missed this.

                        I open my mouth to
                        say the same, but
                        put shortbread there
                                    instead.

It's so easy

to walk out of school at lunchtimes,
    I don't even know
    why I ever stayed in.

Next time,
    Travis gets the chips
    & a Coke for everyone.

79

Safe, I say,
>seeing a glint of gold on his wrist
>as he reaches inside his jacket.

Calm, bro, he says,
>holding out a dripping can.
No sweat.
Cheap as chips!

Maybe the chips were cheap,
>but his watch
>certainly wasn't.

I gotta be honest.

I can see it
>right from the start,
even if mostly
>I choose to look
>the other way.

Some days at the Flo
>are *busy*, if you
>know what I mean.

Seems Travis has
>a lot of calls to make,
>a lot of friends who like to
>drop by just to
>shake his hand.

I'm not stupid.
But it isn't
>my business.

Not yet.

I can hear

a familiar voice
    calling me
    as I head out
    at lunchtime –

Ravi is waving
    from the queue.
Erik! Want me to
    save you a place?
It's battered cod today.

                    I got other fish to fry, my man!
                    I tell him, speeding up.

I hope you know
    what you're doing,
    he says,
not smiling for once.

It's Saturday morning

& it feels waaaaaaay
    too early to wake,
but someone's
    ringing me
    non-stop.

                    I hitch up on my elbow
                    & blink the dream-blur
                    from my eyes.

                    09:23 *WTF?*

                    It's Ravi.

What's the panic, bro?

No panic . . .
Ravi says.
I need to ask a favour,
        that's all.

Uh, sure.
I struggle upright.
Wassup?

Is he serious?

Ravi wants me to meet him at the
        gym-in-the-park
        in the Flo.

I don't wanna be rude, but
I gotta point out,
Ravi, that's really
really not your thing.

Yeah, I know,
        he says.
He sounds sad.
That's the problem.

If the brain

was a muscle,
    Ravi would be a weightlifter.

He's brilliant at chess,
    wins masses of medals.

His dad drives him to competitions:
    whole weekends on the road
    in their battered black Escort.

When I see him beating
    sixth-formers on the chess tables
    in the square,

out-thinking them by miles,
    I think
    my best mate
    might be a genius –

but then he gets up

& trips over
    his laces.

Ravi's got his first

big hots,
    for some Year Eight girl
    called Betty.

She just joined his chess club.
He says she's a
    member of MENSA
    – whatever that is.

He shows me the
    Team Chess Club group photo
    & zooms in.

Betty's solemn-faced: all
    plaits & huge glasses.
The camera doesn't cosy up to her.

She plays the French defence, he says,
sighing like
    she kissed him
    instead of taking his king.

I think she likes me, he says,
pacing the bouncy concrete,
pulling randomly at bars,
but I need her to REALLY
    like me. You know –

LIKE-*like.*

He looks down sadly
    at his soft middle.
I'm not . . . y'know . . .

                           I nod.
                           I know.

. . . I need to
get in shape.

He turns those
    puppy-dog eyes
    on me again.
Will you help me?

                           Me?

I look around at the
outdoor gym, at the
the springs, the weights,
the . . . the . . . *public humiliation*
of it all.

Sure, I say,
watching Ravi step gingerly
onto a tilting board
which w°b_b^le^s him
straight off again.

He covers the moment
with a very bad Elvis impression,
just a boy who
can't help falling in love.

Will I be a coach? he asks.

Shout motivational stuff,
tell him he's amazing?

I say,
*Can't I just stay in bed on FaceTime
& tell you you're amazing
from there?*

Apparently not.
I have to be by his side,
be his
hands-on
personal trainer!

Me? Train Ravi in the Flo,
where everyone
can see us?

This is so
seriously
uncool.

I don't do weights

but I *can* run.

Maybe it's the long legs
    or the Viking blood
    or whatever –
but I'm fast & strong.

In Year Six I got the
    Regional Sprint Championship
    Runner-up Prize.

Dad thought that was
    so funny, he couldn't
    keep his camera still
    for laughing.

> *Ravi*, I say to my friend,
>   putting an arm
> around his padded shoulders,
>   *Ravi, man,*
>   *nothing burns the cals*
>   *like running . . .*

But I've got no idea
    what a bad idea
    this will turn out
    to be.

I suggest we run early,

so no one will spot us –

& Ravi quickly says
    why don't we run his paper round?
He'll give me half.

& then Mum says maybe
    she can earn some cash out cleaning,
    if I jog my sisters back to sleep.

& before I know it, I have been
    totally,
    royally,
    shafted.

Three mornings a week

Mum shrugs into her overalls
    & leaves before light
to clean the loos of strangers
    & wipe the workstations of
    men & women she'll
    never meet.

Three mornings a week
    I'm expected to get up
    at idiot o'clock & stuff
    soft limbs into snowsuits,
    bundle the babies into their buggy.

Not only am I
    running Ravi's paper round,

but the risk
    of ruining my rep.

I have to get up at six.

SIX!

The sun's still low like Laser Quest;
sharp fingers poking into our eyes
    as we head off to the east.

Ravi runs behind the double buggy
passing me the papers to push through
        a hundred knuckle-scraping flaps.

I can't believe
Ravi's been doing this
since he turned twelve
& he's still got all his
    fingers.

Those letter boxes are like
    mantraps, man.
Savage springs.
Sharp edges.

I don't care if it's raining
& the papers turn to pulp
      if they hang outside . . .

I'm not doing it.

Who cares if the shop
      is getting complaints?
Ravi, you gotta *unionise*, bro.

My lovesick friend

walks-runs walks-runs walks-runs
      with no breath
      left for stupid songs.

He's sweating & panting with his
      fringe stuck to his forehead,

blowing raspberries
      at the twins
who are
      laughing up at him –
      him & his jogging suit from Costco.

He is ridiculous, but
      he is determined,

& this Betty'd
      better be
            worth it.

Friday's payday.

Ravi asks Mr Samaan in the shop
     to split the purple banknote
     into two yellow tenners.

                                         Thanks, Ravi!
                                    Total exploitation
                                              but still
                    more money than I've had for months.

                            Lunchtime at the chip shop
                               I offer to pay my way.

Travis takes a peek
     into my wallet & laughs.
Don't sweat it, bro!
Save that for some sweeties
     after school.

He pulls a wad of paper
     from his pocket –
You need to earn yourself
     some
          actual
               cash.

TRAINING

Four weeks into

Ravi's makeover
& we're sitting on a wall to
    catch our breath.

My sweating friend holds out a
    screengrab on his phone.

                                    Huh?
                            A line graph?

Time against weight,
    he explains.
It's working!

It is.
The line is like *a literal ski slope.*

                        Respect. High fives!

My man is indeed looking fitter
    & not so much like
    he's gonna puke his guts up
    with each stride.

He's knocked the Creme Eggs on the head –
    no more freebies at the shop
    (unfortunately for me).

                She givin' you the eye yet, then?

Not yet, says Ravi –
but he smiles, like it's going to plan.
Give it time.

He gets up again.
Come on!

I peel my ass off the wall
reluctantly.
Seriously, man,
how much longer
do we have to do this?

Nothing smells as good as

toast does in the morning.

Back at home
    I'm dolloping fat peanut butter knifefuls
    on slice after slice of toast
while Ravi's cheating his diet with
    a chocolate muffin.

The babies on our laps
    stretch out their chubby fingers.

Uh-uh, not for you!
    Ravi knocks my toast
    out of their reach.
Babies can't have peanuts,
    he explains.

I told you, he knows
    way too much.

Alice grizzles.
I spoon in baby rice.

Ravi checks his phone.
Your mum's normally
    back home by now.
Unlike me, he actually cares
    what time we get to school.

We wait

    & wait
       & w   a   i   t . . .

Mum arrives flustered.
It's all the boss's fault.

She doesn't say thanks.
She doesn't even say sorry.
She just bangs on about me
    finishing the bread.

Talking of which,
    she hasn't even paid me
    for the babysitting.

While I run up garden paths,

hurling papers at doorsteps
    as fast as I can,

I keep an eye open
    for anyone from school,

checking the windows
    of the houses
    for kids eating toast as they dress,
    ready to duck –
but no one
    with any sense is up.

The streets are empty,
    all except the road
    that leads to the park
    which is *rammed* with
    other idiot joggers,

Ravi has to swerve the buggy to & fro making Esme and Alice squeal with excitement.

After a month
    without being spotted by classmates,
    I relax.
Mistake.

I should never
have let down my guard.

One Monday morning

Ravi & I
    are on the home stretch,
running past the Nightingale Estate
& cutting through
    the green bit of the park
    back to the shop.

Ravi's getting faster,
    but I'm way out in front
    as we go past the
    tennis courts –

ERIK! ERIK ANDERSEN!
My name's being bellowed,
    roared like a moose call –
*ERIK! I didn't know
    you were a runner!*

Just my luck.

                            I'm not.
               I look desperately down
              for a pothole in the road
                       wide enough
                      to swallow me.

You could have fooled me,
    says the man in the tracksuit,
    folding his manly arms
    over his manly chest.
I was behind you.
You were making good time!
His beard splits in a Thor-type laugh.
Better than your mate
    with the buggy . . .

We both glance over
    to where Ravi is rocking
a buggyful of squalling babies
    woken by the sudden din.

This games teacher,

Mr Robinson,
    can't be that old,
    but he's old like
    old school.

He's this massive dinosaur
    with a weird beard,

who always wears
    a red-striped tracksuit,
    skanky trainers,
    & a stopwatch.

97

No one has ever –
  ever
  ever
  ever
  seen him dressed in
  anything else.

Ever since Year Seven

I've carefully run
just slow enough
    to stay under Mr Robinson's radar.

I've made sure
    he doesn't pick me for any teams –
but he doesn't pick *on* me either.

I'm not stranded like Ravi, every week
    sitting it out
    on the high-water mark
    of the bench.

But now, after all that work,
    it looks like
    my cover just got blown.

The next day

it's just my luck,
    to have PE first thing.

I am jogging endlessly around & around the orange gravel track, just watching the heels of the person in front of me & wondering how many laps I've done & when it's all going to be over . . .

The air on the field smells smoky, but it's only a groundsman's bonfire; the morning puffers have moved on. A few laps in & I think I'm safely hidden in the middle of the pack when Mr Robinson suddenly goes totally nuclear: *ANDERSEN! STOP PRATTING AROUND & RUN!!!!!!!*

He shouts, *Go!*

as he
    clicks his stopwatch

& doesn't stop yelling,
    FASTER! FASTER!
    for my whole next lap,

like he thinks
    his voice is the key
    to wind me up.

Now he's seen me
    delivering papers,

he won't let me
    deliver less than
    100%.

All week long

– & it's a long, *long* week –

I spend my lunchtimes
    with Mr Robinson
    shouting at me.
Pick your heels up!
Pump your arms
Keep going
    Keep going!
        KEEP GOING!

I run until I'm coughing stars.

He makes me do
    push-ups – air squats – lunges – star jumps
    push-ups – air squats – lunges – star jumps
    push-ups – air squats – lunges – star jumps
    push-ups – air squats – lunges – star jumps
    push-ups – air squats – lunges – star jumps

until I fall flat on my face
    & lie on the track
    with the orange gravel
    painfully freckling my cheek.

Everything hurts.
I want to throw up.

On Friday, on the way back
    to the changing rooms,
    Mr Robinson walks with me
    & I'm just too tired to
    shake him off.

Well done, lad! he says,
Keep it up,
    you're doing great!

In the changing room,

once I've stopped
    wanting to puke,
it's the weirdest thing:

I *feel* great too.

Sort of.

My good mood lasts

for a few days
    until I'm taking the short cut
    through the school square,
head down,
    texting Ravi,

who's spending a study period
    actually *studying*
    & won't answer.

The sun is out. Jumpers are off.
It's starting to smell like summer.

The teachers must have cranked
    the windows open wide
    which is apparent only
    when a missile whistles
        w-h-i-zzzzzzzzzzzzzzzzzzzzzzzzzzzzzzzzzzz

                              SMACK!!!
                             on the back
                          of my head,

knocking me
    & my phone
    flying.

When the sparkly lights
    have cleared
& I can see again,

a water bottle's rolling
    on the paving,
    right next to my
    totally shattered
    phone.

Someone calls out,
Gin-ger-nut!

& a window's hastily
    pulled shut.

It's not hard

to find out
    whose idea of a joke
    that was.

Harry Bateman in Year Ten.

Thinks he's so hard
    but he's a *knob* –

& in the lunch queue
    I smack him
    round his fat head
    to say so.

Fighting might not
    get me
    a new phone

but I did get
    a lot of satisfaction

– & another
    visit to the Blue Room.

Ben & Travis are already

tucked into their usual booths.

Do they even bother going to class?

My left eye's closing
so I wink them
with my right.

who won?
    asks the note
    that drops on my desk.

Harry Bastard Bateman
I send back –

though as it turns out,
he's a loser.

Harry Bastard Bateman

doesn't come to school
for the rest of that week.

Rumour has it
    he met with an accident
    on his way home:

he got jumped by
    two guys in hoods:
        one tall,
        one short,

both completely
    unidentifiable.

I'm sorry, boys.

That Friday morning
Mr Samaan gives us a
    disapproving tongue-cluck.
This is for last week
    & then that's it.
I don't want you doing the round.
Too many wet papers.
Too many complaints.
Bad for my business.

The bell jangles as we leave.
It's started to drizzle &
    I pull the cover
    over my sleeping sisters.

Ravi runs away so fast

                              I have to leg it
                                to catch him up.
                          I tap his shoulder.
                              Be cool, man.
                    I mean, it was shit pay,
                              anyway, right?

But he shakes my hand off,
& when he whirls round
    his glasses are misted up.
You promised you were
    doing it properly!
My dad'll be furious!

He jogs away from me,
fury lifting up his heels.

                              I shrug.
                          So, I lied.

In the Flo at lunch,

Travis flattens his stub
   on the bouncy concrete.

Can't be arsed to go back to school now, man.
Let's go to the mall.
   He gets up &
   lets the swing squeal back.
I fancy some trainers
   from the sports shop.

In the mall
   the sound of heels & babies crying
   bounces sharply off the shiny floor,
but it's Thursday afternoon
   & most kids
   are in school –

where I should be too,
   but this is so much
   more fun
   than a history test.

The sports shop has

rows & rows & rows &
rows & rows & rows &
   rows & rows & rows &
   rows & rows & rows &
rows & rows & rows &
   rows & rows & rows

of trainers I can't afford.

The boy who serves us

looks exhausted before we start.

Travis & Ben get him
    running back & forth
    about a hundred times
    before
    they each pick out a pair of
    Nikes that cost
    more than twice
    what I spend in SaverMart
    in a week.

What about you, bro?
    asks Ben, looking down
    at my school shoes.
You don't want nothin'?

                       It's hard to
                 shake my head,
because it isn't just the trainers:

                     I want so much.

I'll get you a pair,

says Travis,
& even though
    I know he must be joking,
still I let them send the boy
    to hunt me down
    Adidas in size eight.

Here! says Travis, while he's gone,
    passing me a pair of
    flash black Nikes.
Slip these on, quick.
Put your school shoes
    in your bag.

                The trainers fit so snug
                 & they look so good,
          Like they belong on my feet.
               I want them *so bad*.

We're standing

in the short line to the till
& my heart is thumping,
    battering its way outta my ribs
& the boy comes back
& Travis says, *Sorry, man,*
    we changed our minds, innit,
& we're at the front of the line
& they're forking out
    mad thick wads of tenners
& I'm staring at the socks
& not at anybody's eyes
& we're walking out, those
    beautiful Nikes on my feet,
they're leading me out
& we're almost at the door
& we've made it, we've done it,
& the guard's not even looking, he –

Travis stops.
Swings round.
Points at my feet.
ERIK, MATE!
WHAT YOU DOIN'?
YOU STEALIN' THEM CREPS, BRO?

& everyone –
I mean, *everyone* –
    turns to stare
    at me.

All the way out

of the mall,
Travis & Ben are pissing themselves
    laughing.

                                        I still feel sick.

Your face, man!
    says Ben, for about the
    hundredth time.

                                It's not funny.
                    I thought I was actually
                            going to chuck
            when the security guard's head
                        snapped round &
                    Travis shoved me back
                        towards the till.

I'm so sorry, miss,
  he told the girl
  politely.
My friend forgot
  he had them on.

Then he just
  pulled out his wallet
  & paid.

The underpass

smells of piss, like always.

Travis's face flickers
  in the busted light.
He's still grinning.
Ben too.
Ben tells me to be cool:
  it was just for a laugh.

Travis says,
Money's not a problem, man,
I always got plenty.

He puts his hand on my arm.
They're yours,
  he says.
No sweat.

But I can feel the wet
circles
spreading
under my arms.

Mum's standing

in the kitchen doorway
    when I get home from school.

The trainers will have to
    stay in my bag
    until I've thought up a
    cover story.

I try to dodge past
    but she blocks my way,
    a twin hitched on each hip.
Her face is set hard, her
    nostrils white, lips tight.
I got an email
    from the school today.
Where were you?

> *Somewhere else*,
> I say.
> I take the stairs
> two at
> a time
> & ignore her
> telling me to

Come back here!
We haven't finished!

> because as far as I'm concerned,
> we have.

111

We always have a deal.

When Mum upgrades,
I get her old phone.

But now she's holding up
　　some crappy old brick
& telling me
　　she had to
　　sell her good one on.

*It was the phone
　　or the gas bill,*
　　she says.

I don't care if we
　　need the money –
　　she broke a promise.

Right now
　　I hate her
　　nearly as much
　　as I hate Harry Bateman.

K1

It's Sunday

& Ravi's still keeping up
    the radio silence,
    sulking about his
    stupid paper round.

Mum & I aren't talking either –

but the bonus is she doesn't
    ask me to do stuff,

so I have a lie-in
    before I head off to the Flo.

I'm going nuts

without a phone.

On the ten-minute
    walk to the Flo
    I must've grabbed for it
    maybe twenty times.

It's like that thing
    I heard about,
    how amputees
    still scratch their missing limbs.

The Flo

is almost empty
    bar some teenies
    on the slide.

With no phone
    I just sit on a bench
    & count the dog craps
    till Travis comes strolling
    through the arch.

Y'all right, Erik my man?
We fist-bump & I spot
    new metal on his wrist.
He sees me looking
    & flexes.
Nice, eh? Too nice
    to wear for school, innit?

                               Yeah.
                   It must've cost a load.
                       Where's Ben?

He's comin', bro.
Travis nods at a white
BMW just nudging into the kerb.

Ben gets out one side.
    & the driver
    unfolds himself
    from the other.

Even taller than Ben
with a dark jacket,
    his hair & beard cropped so short
    you can't at first tell
    he's a redhead like me –

but you can't miss
the tear-track scar, twisting down his cheek into a sneer.

The park gate clangs
    as the kids on the slide
    decide to
    make an exit,

like they spotted a shark
    in the water.

I'm hanging back.

Travis never mentioned
    meeting up with mates –
just said to be here,
    don't be late.

They bump fists like bloods.

Travis pushes me forward
    then steps back.

You're Erik, yeah?
The guy with the scar
    looks me
        up
        &
        down
as if he's buying.

                        Who is this dude?
        I cross my arms like I ain't scared.
                        Yeah. Who're you?

Travis steps in, quick.
Calm, Posh Boy.
Erik, meet Kei Wun.
He thinks he can do
*   you a favour.*

Kei Wun?

Kay wun?

       Kay One?

K1?

What kinda
    weird-ass name
    is that?

One thing's for sure:
I'm not gonna ask.

The sneer

turns into a smile.

Hello, Posh Boy.
I hear you're not so posh.
I hear your phone got broke –
K1 shakes his head in sympathy –
    & you ain't got the paper
    for another.

I can see the sunlight
catching fire in his hair
& glinting off a
gold eye tooth.

Bet no one calls *him* Gingernut.

Travis says your dad died.
He says you gotta
    be the man in your yard.
That's peak, man.
Tough.

K1 knows a bunch of my business.
I throw Travis a
what-the-heck? look, but
he refuses to catch it.

K1 steps in close –
    very close,
    like he's gonna ask me to dance –
He says you might be into
    earning some cash.
That right, bro?

His breath is in my face now,
    & I can definitely
    smell the coffee.

I know

you think this is it,
    this is the *when* –
    & yeah, of course
    it is.

Kinda.

This is the moment
    I had the choice:
    yes or no.

But.

Not making excuses,
but it was
    all the stuff before,
    all those other dominoes
    leaning on my back.

That's what *tipped me over.*

K1 & me

are sitting at the picnic table
    in the corner of the rec.

The wooden slats are
    warped & broken,
    slimy.

All you gotta remember
    says K1, looking me
    square in the eye,
    is you bring me back
    the right money,
        every
        single
        time.

I stare back & all I can see
is that puckered slash
slicing up his face.

Is that a knife scar?

A news ticker talks
across the bottom of my brain:

Is it too late to change my mind? Is it too late to change m

Like he can read it,
    K1 punches my shoulder.
    Calm, no pressure.
    Right, Erik? Right?

                                    Right. I nod.

You'll be makin' Ps.
You'll be cool,
    shottin' for me.

                                    I nod again
                                    & run my thumbnail
                            into the soft rot of the table,
                    across the green groove of the grain.

You look after us

& we'll look after you, right?
K1 passes me the joint.

His Zippo flame flickers
    in a gust of March wind.
The swings twist & moan a little
    on their chains.

We're all family here,
    even a posh boy like you –
    ain't that so, Ben?
    he says to Ben, who nods.

Travis & Ben, they're like
    your cousins now, innit?
        You keep each other close.

But cousin Travis has wandered off.
    At the arch he greets a skinny
    stooping girl with black dreads
    hanging down her back.

They do the handshake thing
    & she's away.

K1 hooks a thumb in their direction.
See how easy it is, bro?
You just gotta bring back
    the right paper & –
    & this one's real important –
He leans across the table,
his dead-shark eyes hooked into mine.
DON'T . . . GET . . . CAUGHT.

A sudden change of mood
& he flashes the gold tooth
& laughs.
I know you won't get caught, bro,
    cos Travis says you're clever.
Face it, if Ben's doin' okay,
it can't be that hard, right?

His laughter feels fine,
    like family.

Just joking.
No harm.

K1 is halfway

to his car & I'm stood
    watching his back,
    thinking, *Is that it?*
when he wheels round –
    Here! he says.

From his pocket
    he pulls a box & throws it   up   up   up
    against the violet sky.

                    I dive for it. It's a Lyca.

That's just a burner
    for selling the food, man.
But this one's for you.

He steps forward,
    feels in the other pocket
    & passes another phone to me
    as gently as he would
    an eggbox.

This is on account.
You understand?
You'll work it off.

                    For the first time,
                      I let myself
                      smile at him.

                    Safe, I say.

Up in my room

I put my new
    phone on charge.

It fits into my palm
    snug as a
    prosthetic
    on a stump.

It might not be
    new-new . . .

It might not be
    the latest . . .

But it sure is an
    upgrade
    for me.

All those mornings,

before it all went wrong,

Dad coming in
    from the early shift,
    pale with tiredness
    even under his dusting
    of bakery flour,

a faint whiff of cinnamon buns
    clinging to his whites,

Mum stood behind him,
kneading out
    the knots that had been
    kneaded in.

He was
    man of the house.

Now it's my turn.

LIES

Mum comes in from the garden,

dumps the laundry,
starts mixing baby rice.

Look, Mum, look!
I show her the phone.
Look what Jordan Ikes gave me!

I tell her
Jordan got an upgrade
& passed his old one on –
Jordan Ikes lives by the river;
his folks are loaded.

She's so busy spooning
   rice into my sisters
   she swallows it
   without question.

That's so nice of him,
   she says, watching the
rice slip down
   as easily as
   my lies.

I haven't told mum

that I lost Ravi
   his paper round.

On Monday morning at six
   I still get the steam
   from a cuppa
   tickling my nose.

She puts on her overalls
    & kisses the girls goodbye
    as sunlight inches across
    the kitchen floor.

Esme opens & closes
    her fat little fist in a
    cute anemone wave.

Mum rushes out
    without noticing
    that Ravi should be here
    by now.

Mum wrote down

the new number
    for her dumb phone
& asked me to give it to the school office
    so they can ring her
    to rat on me.

Not the smartest of moves,
to be honest.

And now she doesn't
    get her email on her phone,
    it's piss-easy to
    hack into her account
    on the ancient desktop.

I'm so sorry about Erik's attitude,
    I type, as I listen to
    Mum bathing the babies
    upstairs. Splashes. Squeals.

I'm sure you appreciate he's not having an easy time
    right now . . .

I sign & send & set up a filter
    to forward emails
    from the school so they
    skip her inbox altogether.

Like K1 said – I'm clever.

I tell

Ben & Travis
    I have to train
    most lunchtimes.

Just don't turn up, bro!
    says Travis,
    already heading to the gate.

Yeah, he can't make you!
    Ben trails along
    in Travis's wake.
It's extra curr-cur— it's extra, innit?

                    I don't want to tell them
                        how much I like
                the way that running makes me feel.
        The way that being *good* at running makes me feel.

                        So I just shrug.
                    He'll put me on report
                        if I don't show,
                            I lie.

I thought Ravi

would maybe
    come & watch me train,
    but he says no, that he & Betty
    are working on
    their *opening moves*.

                      & I say, *Whatever*.

Mum says

Just tell me where you are,
    so I won't worry.

                      If I told her
                where I really was,
                she'd never stop.

          I'm going over Jordan's –
                that okay? I say,
                super casual,
       shrugging on my hoodie
                after tea.

Okay, Mum says,
    head inside the dishwasher.
Not at Ravi's tonight?

                      Nah, I say
      & shut the door on her muffled

Don't be late!

You can see it, can't you?

All the lies I'm telling . . .
    they're starting to fester,
to wriggle like maggots
    in the food bin.

K1 leaves the engine running,

the dashboard glowing like a
    games console, the
    engine ticking softly,
    tut-tut-tut-tut.

Here.
He passes a backpack.
I look inside to see
    a bag of little bags.

You betta count them,
    he says, suddenly all
    maths teacher.
& you betta get it right.
Tell me how much cash
    you gotta give me back.

I do the maths
& it's not hard –

It looks like
easy money
to me.

May 21st is

Dad's birthday (*was* Dad's birthday).
Mum's putting on lipstick
    & a brave face.

The twins are la-la-la-ing in their buggy,
    ready to roll,
cos today's no big deal to them.

Mum tells me
    the bluebells are out
    on his grave.

She says it's pretty.
She says it's a lovely day.
She says *please* won't I visit with her,
    just this once?

Won't I wish him happy birthday?
Tell him what I've been
up to?

                        No I won't.
                          I *can't.*

                        Not gonna lie
                             to Dad.

Thunk!

The stress ball
hits the wall
a touch to the side
of Dad's smile.

Thunk!

His arm round my
eleven-year-old shoulders,
my grin covered in
his (last-ever) birthday cake.

Thunk!

Maybe it's time to
rearrange my room
so Dad's photo isn't quite so
much in my face?

Thunk!
Thunk!
Thunk!
Thunk!

It's a relief when a call comes
& I can be out when
Mum gets back.

Yo! Viking Line!

Time to feed the cats.

CATS

I go fishing

in the city's stagnant pools,
    wading in the murkiest waters,
    casting out my
    Viking Line.

My hook is baited
    with words:
Need anything, mate?

Later, when my
    burner buzzes,

I know
   I've got
    a bite.

The thing about Jordan Ikes

is that he lives
    waaaaaaaaaaaaaay over
    the other
    side of town,
    in the posh houses
    by the station.

Unlike Ravi, whose
    house is so close that
    my mum bumps into
    his dad out shopping
    every other day.

I text Mum:
Staying at Jordan's, K?

Jordan Ikes's family
    are very kind indeed,
    the way they let me
    crash at theirs
    whenever it gets late –

Jordan Ikes himself
    of course,
    has no idea
    how close
    he & I
    have gotten.

The money

isn't easy though –
    not as easy as I thought.

There's nothing easy about
    standing like an almost

invisible pillar in the dark, the
    moon shining off the eyes of

my alleycats as they come
    skulking, slinking, stinking
    up to me, one by one.

A'ight, mate,
    they whisper
    to me in the
    rustling dark,

rubbing knuckles
    for their food.
A'ight.

One by One
the calls come
in & the deal
is done.
All night long
the dealing's done:
how hungrily the cats
come hunting for their
grub under the moon:
they call me & they
come, one
                    by
                          one
                                by
                          one
              by one.

Tucked into a corner

of the Flo
    a little brick shed squats behind
    a tangle of brambles.

Mum told me it used to be a chapel
    where parents would pray
    for their sick kids,

& it became
    a gardener's hut,
    a safe place
    to lock away the tools.

But now the padlock is busted,
    & the roof opens up to the sky,

& nettles & ivy grow over the
    litter of bottles & needles
    like camouflage.

I have to
    wrinkle my nose
    against the smell inside,
    but at least I'm

                                         hidden.

I'm done.

Crouched at the back
    of the shed
    I'm counting more money
    than I've ever had before
    except in Monopoly –

but this is for real:
    this ain't
    no game.

The moon slides behind a cloud
    & the white BMW shark-glides
    to the kerb.

> I've gotta have
> every last fiver
> accounted for
> or
> I can count
> myself dead –

the man with the scar
would feed me
    to the fishes.

> It's cold
> but I'm sweating.

My phone pings.
    READY 4 PICK-UP?

> I type
> with fingers
> stiff from cold:
> *OK*

The whirr of the window

& K1's voice
Don't just stand there –
      get in, quick!

Inside, the passenger seat
      is warm against my
      dawn-chilled
      legs.

K1 holds out his hand
      without a word.

He opens the bag with a
riiiiiiiiiiiiiiiiiiip
& I think he's
      unzipped my ribs
      so my heart
      can burst right through.

Did I take the right money?
Did I get it right?
Did I? *Did I?*

In the glow from the dash
      K1 counts as quickly
      as the woman in
      the post office
      whose thin lips move
      like she's praying.

I think of all those
      grubby notes slipped into my
      sweating palm,
all those folded fivers.

Now it's me
      who's praying.

K1 closes the bag

& nods his head in a
    quick duck-dip
    of approval.

His scar
    wrinkles
    into a smile.

All good.

K1 pulls out some
    notes & fans them
    across my face.
*Just a few, cos you're
    earnin' back your phone still,
    a'ight, bro?*

> I stuff the paper
> into my pocket
> before he can change
> his mind.

Smart boy,
    he says.
*Call me when you want
    some more.*

Well done.

I sit on my bed

to count
my earnings.

The smell of bud
    wafts off the paper
    sickly as Magic Tree
    car freshener.

The last time anyone
    put money in my hand
    & said, *Well done*
    was my dad
    when I washed his motor.

Well, Dad –

I slide the notes into a ziplock
    & tuck them
    safely away

You'd have gotten
five *clean cars*
for this.

141

It's not only

Travis, Ben & me
    hanging out on the streets
    doing what we do.

K1's got other troops
    to hold the ground,
    to stake his claim.

This slice of the city
    is theirs.

I'm getting to know them,
    these roadmen,
    so sure,
    so much older than me,
    dressed like kings.

They welcome me.
I can tell by their easy shouts
    across the street –
Yo! Erik!
    What you sayin'?
        You chillin' wid man today?

I wouldn't call us *family*,
    not exactly –
    but close.

We're close.

So many rules

to learn.

Sometimes I feel
    like I'm starting school
    all over again

learning
    where I can go
    who I can talk to
    what I can do where.

If you make a mistake
    you learn the hard way.

Some of the roadmen
    have tattoos to show their tribe,

some have scars . . .

Like Nathan.

Nathan's an elder,
one of K1's *bloods*
with a stick'n'poke under his eye –
five dots like a dice –
& Air Max bright as a
butterfly wing.

He wanders into the Flo
    one Friday afternoon.

Wassup?
You guys comin' over
    the house, man?

He slings an arm
    round my shoulders.
It's Friday.
Who wants to be at school
    on a Friday afternoon?

Not me.

Never mind
    that I should be sitting
    my assessments right now.

Never mind
    that I should be choosing
        my future career path.

I choose
    to follow
    my new friends down the path to the Nightingale Estate.

Up & down my hilly street

the terraced houses link arms &
    lean against each other for support.

They're
scared
to face the local estate,
the Nightingale,
with its graffitied walkways
        &
row after row of scruffy doors –
    so many patched with

the chipboard squares that tell
    the story of a kicking,

like a face with a
    faded bruise.

Gotta be honest

I haven't been to the Nightingale
    a whole lot.
If you don't actually live there,
    you don't.

There are maybe
    five or six big brick blocks,
    striped like a cake
    with layers of concrete icing.

Travis & Ben seem to know
    their way, leading us
    past scrubby bushes,
    a half-arsed
    attempt at green.

A'ight, big man?
You ready for
    another pack?
I walk with Nathan.
He lives here.

That's my mum's.
He points at a first-floor flat
    nicer than most,
    plants & flowers everywhere
    like a crown crammed with jewels.
She's mad for her balcony.

Where we're walking,
    under the unloved bushes,
    cans & bottles,
    needles & wrappers,
    sprout up like weeds.

At the flat

I'm careful not to stare

into the kitchen,
    where a girl
    not much older than me
    lifts a yellow hank of hair
    to chase the powder
    disappearing into her face
      like the tail of a little white mouse

at the corner of the living room,
    the bony form curled like a fossil
    in a filthy sleeping bag;
    a shape which only coughs & stirs
    when Nathan nudges him
    with his Air Max.
        Rocko! Still here,
        you prick?

at the low glass table filmy with ash & littered with cups & cans
& fag ends & scales & blades & Vaseline & cartons & lighters
& a bong & pills & three great big jam jars & maybe a dozen
or so little baggies all packed with the best quality green bud.

K1 is on the sofa counting.
He points for me & Nathan to sit
    so I perch beside him on the
    dirty cushions in a patch of
    murky sunlight filtered
    through the nets.

Travis & Ben
    stay with the girl in the kitchen.
    They're laughing.

Drill music
    punctures the wall.

Nathan gets out a pouch
    & starts to roll

& Travis hands me the scales
    & some bags
    & tells me to get going.

It's Friday afternoon,
& I'm just chillin'.

Chillin' with my fam.

The blonde girl's

Nathan's girlfriend.
We're in the kitchen.
I'm making coffee.

She's a few years older than me,
in tight black jeans &
    a pink crop top.

I flick my eyes down, quickly.
        Chantelle is tattooed
over her navel
    in loopy blue.

Rocko! she calls out
        to the bundle
        in the corner of the
        living room.
*I'm picking up your pension,
        right, man?*

The fossil moans & coughs
        but makes no other
        sound.

                    Would he like a coffee?
                    I ask, hand poised
                        over the jar.

Chantelle stops, looks surprised,
        then smiles.
*Prob'ly tip it all over hisself,
        but yeah, he would, I s'pect.*

Heading out the door,
she calls back –
Don't make it too hot!

I'm on my way back home,

timing my return
for the end of school,
kicking a can down the

weedy alleyway

which runs like a firebreak
along the edge of the estate.

Hey, Posh Boy!

I look up & it's Chantelle,
a massive bag of shopping
heavy as a child in her arms.

A hand, please?
She gives me a Coke
& not much choice.

Retracing my steps,
I pluck up the courage to ask her
the question that's been bugging me.
So how come
K1 lets Rocko live in his flat?

Chantelle laughs like that's
the best joke she's heard in years,
but I can't figure out
what's funny.

Trap house.

Trap. House. House trap.
Rocko's been cuckooed.

K1's taken over
    the old man's nest.

It's not so bad,
she says,
& taps her nose.

He gets what he needs.
I look out for him.

BOXES

Word about

the Viking Line
    spreads like a virus.

I'm busy
    day & night

        cutting | weighing | folding | sealing | *running*

Tired, yeah –
    but
    learning to
    deal with it.

Putting money in my pocket

is like sucking in air.
I'm just *gulping* it.

By the end of June
    it feels like
    finally I can breathe –

like poverty's taken
    its sweaty hand
    off my mouth.

In shops I exhale
    cautiously. I don't
    let it out
    all at once.

Compartmentalisation

is a Ravi word
  for keeping all the
  different bits
  of your life in
  different boxes

& keeping the boxes
  locked shut.

Man, I've got
  way too many
  bits in boxes.

How do I keep my
  shit together
& all the different
  boxes far apart?

Although they threaten to split open . . .

Or run or deal
When it's lunch, I
train around the
track or trade my
pack, depends . . .

run or deal or run or deal or

Ravi Ravi Ravi Ravi

& Ravi walks with
Betty these days –
doesn't talk to me
so much, which is
(tbh) less awkward.

Ravi Ravi Ravi Ravi Ravi Ravi Ravi Ravi Ravi Ravi Ravi Ravi Ravi

Esme & Alice & Esme &

. . . but mostly it's a
jog round the block
until the twins drop
off, then back to bed
to catch more zzzzz

& Alice & Esme & Alice & Esme & Alice & Esme & Alice

deal deal deal deal

Sometimes I help
out a cat or two:
some hungry fella
been up mewing
all night through

deal deal deal deal deal deal deal deal deal deal deal deal

Mum Mum Mum

On days Mum
works I still get
up early & make
like I'm running
with my mate.

Mum Mum Mum Mum Mum Mum Mum Mum Mum

or run

food food food
food food food
food food food
At home I hang
around just long
enough to eat my
tea, then back on
the street for me.
food food food

. . . there's one lid I keep tightly shut:

Dad Dad Dad
Dad Dad Dad
Dad Dad Dad
Dad Dad Dad
Dad Dad Dad
Dad Dad Dad
Dad Dad Dad

One night

a call comes in
& I ride out
    to the fancy houses
    with their backs to the river.

Even from the other side,
I can tell which one it is –
every window's glowing welcome,
like an Advent calendar
    on Christmas Eve.

The tunes leaking out
    across the lawn
    could come from a
    Ravi playlist, they're so old.

I cross the bridge,

& watch the slice of light
    widen across the doorway

Hello? Are you there? Hello?
    A woman looking for her knight
    with the white charger.

Hooded & head down,
    I pass across my pack of party fun,
count the cash & nod *okay.*

I'm not hanging around for a tip
from Jordan Ikes's mother.

It's Friday night

& it's pelting down, the rain is brutal.
I've made good wedge this week, –
don't need to wreck
        my trainers in the wet.

                              I sit in the kitchen,
                              feet in socks on the table.

Mum's washing the day's long queue
        of bottles at the sink.

Out of the blue, she says,
        *D'you remember
        Friday nights with Dad?*

                              Memory rushes in
                              like a flood of saliva.

                              Takeouts & telly.
                              Fighting over the remote.
                    That time when me & Dad had
                    a massive prawn fight. The *laughs.*

                              I swallow.
                              It's been a long time.

Mum's mouth starts
        twisting out of shape.

                              I can't think
                              about Dad, I can't –

Let's get a curry! I say quickly,
                pulling out my wallet
                & pushing the lid back down
                on thoughts of Dad.

                              I'll take care of it.

157

Feels good to be the one

making the order,
    taking the delivery.

The dripping guy holds up a soggy bag:
    One chicken madras, one prawn tikka masala ,
    two garlic naans, one pilau rice &
    a bottle of Coke.

Wow!
Mum's sneaked behind me
    as I open up my wallet.
She sees the flash of the cash.
All those newspapers sure add up,
    she says,
        like she wants to say more.

                                        I stow the Ps
                                    & hustle quickly
                            past her with the grub.
                            This smells amazing!

But chicken madras

doesn't taste
    the same
        without Dad.

Or maybe it's
    the way
        Mum's looking at me

that's putting me off my food.

I know Mum is

starting to suspect,
the way she sniffs the air
   when I walk in.

When she opens her mouth
   to ask, *Erik* –
  I just walk out.

                             Got places to be.

She's stopped even asking
   what time I'll be home.

I know she's wondering.

But wondering
   isn't the same as *knowing*,
  is it?

You can fool yourself
   a long time

if you try.

Mr Choudhri's

accidentally
    dropped me in it.

Mum comes in from shopping
    one day
    & makes a cup of tea
    the size of a swimming pool.

Always a bad sign.

I head out, but she calls me back
    & tells me to sit down –
            NOW.

She bumped into Ravi's dad
    who told her what a shame it was
    we don't do the paper round
    these days.

Mum shoots questions at me faster
    than sniper fire –
I'm ducking & weaving
    but it's hard not to get hit.

She threatens to lock the doors
    & windows
    & take away my mobile
    & my trainers
    & my keys

unless she gets
    some answers.

Luckily I've got some covering fire prepared.

Why did you lie about the paper round?

Ravi & I had a row.
I didn't want you gossiping with his dad,
like you always do.

Where did you get the money for the meal?

There's a guy at school.
His dad was giving him hell about his grades, so
I wrote some essays for him.
I wanted to give you a treat.
Excuse me for trying to be nice.

Why do you come in stinking of grass?

So I smoke a little weed sometimes?
Everyone does, if you haven't noticed.
It helps.

With what? What does it help with?

Defence isn't working. Time to return fire.

With you, Mum.
It helps with YOU!

It's a direct hit.
There's a long pause while Mum
recovers & reloads.

Why do you stay at Jordan Ikes's all the time?

So I can do my homework in peace.
Because you spend half the time crying, &
– if you really want to know, Mum –
*because **his** mother*
takes care of me.

Harsh, I know.

& (mostly) lies.

But I tell myself
    it's for her own good –
I'm protecting my mum from the truth.

Sometimes you gotta
    be cruel
      to be kind.

SCHOOL

Can't lie, man,

it gets dull sometimes,
hanging around in the Flo
    all by yourself,
waiting for calls.

                        I watch the sun rise & set.
           I watch the kids swing back & forth.
             I watch the folk go in & out
             of the chip shop on the corner.

One Saturday, a girl sits on the wall
    eating from a cardboard box &
    swinging her skinny legs.

Younger than me. Dark-skinned,
    a bobble hat over plaited pigtails &
    glasses too big for her face.
Familiar.

Her head nods up & down
    as she eats & stares at me –

        down – scoff
        up – stare
        down – scoff
        up – stare.

                        It's weird. Off-putting.
                    I try to stare her out
              until a cat comes calling.
           When I look up again,
                        she's gone.

A minute later, a voice from behind me
calls, *Erik Andersen!* It's
a girl's voice, high & clear.

Erik Andersen!

I know who you are
    & what you're doing
        & you're need to STOP!

                        As the girl with the bobble hat
                                    exits the park,
                                the penny drops.

                                            Betty.

Some nights

Ben & Travis share
    the Viking Line
    with me.

Most nights we also
    share a smoke
    or two, just
    to pass the time,

while the mangy alley cats
    creep in & creep away
    on brittle legs,

looking real bad
& smelling real worse.

One night, Travis
    offers me a line or two of white
to help me while away the night.

I pass.

I need to stay fit

now Mr Robinson's got
    his kettlebell-size
    hands on me.

ANDERSEN! he shouts –

    he always shouts,
    he hasn't got
    an indoor voice –

YOU CAN
    BE BETTER THAN THIS!

> I want to shout back
> *This is as good as*
>   *I get!*
> but I need all my breath
>   to run.
>
> When I'm running,
> my head is clear & clean.
>
> I'm a pure conversion of energy
>   chemical ——> kinetic
>
> I'm a force.
> I'm a power.
> I'm supersonic.
>
> I don't need
> any other
> kind of speed.

No one's allowed to run

in the corridors at school,
not even runners
        like me.

I've been
    avoiding him,
but at lunch today, Ravi races
    after me & I can't
    get away.

He grabs my arm.
    Erik!
    Stop!
    I want to talk to you!

Why can't Ravi just

                                    Back off!

Actually why can't he just

                                    Get lost!

altogether,
    go listen to his
    weirdo suck-ass music
    with his brainy
    blabbermouth
    girlfriend?

                            Just leave me alone.

Stop making me
    feel guilty.

If I'd punched my best mate

with my fists instead of words
he couldn't have
     looked more shocked.

I can't tell him *sorry*
     because these days
     I can't tell him
     anything
     at all.

I panic

& fling open the door
     to an empty classroom
     on my right.

Our form room
     as it happens.

I don't expect Ravi
     to come in after me:
we're not allowed
     in classrooms during break,

& Ravi follows rules
     like they're cat's eyes
     down the
     motorway of life.

This is ridiculous!

Ravi's breathing hard
as he closes the door
    behind us.
Stop acting like a child!
I'm not your mum!

Actually, he sounds
    just like my mum
    right now.

He walks towards me

                               & I back away.

I just want to know
    what's going on with you,
      that's all. Tell me the truth.
What're you up to, Erik?

The door handle creaks & turns.

                             I dive into the
                                  nar
                                  row
                                  gap
                    between the lockers
                         & the window.

It's tight as a tourniquet in here:
    my cheek's squished up
    against the sun-hot glass.

Ravi Choudhri!
Mrs Raynor's voice
    could cut glass.
Just WHAT d'you think
    you're doing in here?

Silence.

Yes?

Well, the thing is . . .
Ravi clears his throat.
*Erik said he threw my book
    behind the lockers.*

                    Well, thanks
            a whole bunch, mate.

Ravi's face appears
    through the gap.

So, is it there? Mrs Raynor asks.

                    I give him
             my fat finger.

He scowls at me.
No, miss.
He must've been lying.

Mrs Raynor sighs.
*Well, it wouldn't be
    the first time Erik's told a lie,
    now, would it?*
Perhaps –
the door handle creaks again –
*you need to choose your friends
    more carefully.*

Off you go to lunch, now.

I'm stuck there for thirty minutes

while Mrs Raynor
    eats her sandwiches.

My ears are on fire,
    not only from the sun:

on the path outside the window
    a crowd of kids has gathered
    to mock the display
    dummy.

By the time she leaves the room,
I'm a laughing stock.

Mrs Raynor

takes her glasses off
    when she's angry,
as if she just can't stand
    to bring us into focus.

When she calls me over
    at registration that afternoon,
she snaps them *shut!*
    in their red leather case
& I know I'm in trouble
    for sure.

Erik. A word, please.
She's definitely fuming,
blinking fury in morse code
    through her wispy fringe.

Well, I'm not exactly
thrilled with her either,
after spending most of lunch like a
zoo specimen.

I saunter to her desk
& fold my arms.
Yeah. What?

Mrs Raynor asks
if it's true I've been
leaving school at lunchtimes.

I say,
*No, miss,
of course not.*

Mrs Raynor asks
if I think she's
some kind of idiot –

& I take
the fifth amendment.

Mrs Raynor says
my place on the school trip is
under consideration.

& I say,
*Yes, miss.
No, miss.*

Mrs Raynor doesn't miss my eyeroll.

I don't care
about the letter
she's sending home:

I'm always first past the post
in the mornings.

I'm late for French

& Monsieur Lebron forces me to say
   how *désolé* I am for being *en retard*,
   before snapping, *Assieds-toi!*

The only empty seat
   is in the back row,
   next to Ravi.

You're going to get yourself
   into real trouble, he hisses.

        So? Since when's it
          your business?

I just don't get why
   you hang out with that pond-life!
His whisper is so preachy
   I could puke.
They're scum, Erik.
They're just using you!
Can't you see that?

        Well, no one disses my friends –
          not even my friends.

           Well, for a start,
       they're more fun than you!
           I hiss back
             to my

           ex-ami.

At the next team training

Mr Robinson's whistle
   Pheeeeeeeeps

& Anu Ganguli –

twice officially crowned
   400m under-sixteens
   Regional Champion Sprinter
& forever the unofficial King
   of the Holland Road Track Team –

is first away like always,
skinny legs & pointy elbows
   spiking up the track.

But today, it's different:
maybe it's the row with Ravi or
   maybe the run-in with my tutor,
but today I'm gaining,
I'm actually gaining on him,
I'm closing the gap.

He's only in my sight
   for seconds before
   he's history behind my
   turbo-powered heels.

I've hit my stride;
   he's in my dust;
I'm like a rocket, man,
   don't stop me now –

I can't get rid of
   Ravi's earworms,
but at least they power me
   across the line.

Mr Robinson

steps in from the side,
    holding his stopwatch
    out like a medal.

                    I'm whooping in air
                     & there's an evil
                        stitch still
        chewing through my side:
        I can't even straighten up
                   to check my time.

UNDER SIXTY SECONDS!
NOT BAD, ANDERSEN!
NOT BAD AT ALL!
the human tannoy
    booms across the field.

Anu comes loping over,
    breathing hard,
    sweating harder.
Well done, mate!

He claps my back
    & my overheated heart
    swells a little more
    at this applause
    from royalty.

I've got plans for you, my lad,

says Mr R,
    watching me
    stretch my tightened muscles
    in the break.

What you did back there –
    he gestures at the track –
    you can do again.
I'm entering you
    for the four hundred
    in the district heats.

                      You are?
                  I blink the sweat
                  out of my eyes.

I am. So I'll see you here
at 8 a.m. every day
next week.

                      But that's –

Half-term. Exactly.
No lessons to distract you.

And – he's gone,
his massive figure
    shrinking as he
    stomps back to
    the school.

                  No chance of an
        'Is that okay with you, Erik?'

                  I told you, didn't I?
                  Mr Robinson?
                  Old school.

Mum's totally thrilled

about the Districts.

She even bakes a cake
& smears a melted Mars Bar
    on the top, like a birthday treat –
it's the babies' first taste of chocolate.

                              I text Ravi a picture, which

he accepts as the peace offering it is.
Haha, look at their eyes!
They look like tarsiers!

                              I google 'tarsiers'
                                & he's right.

Erik, that's amazing!
    Mum keeps saying.

It makes me happy
but it also makes me think
    how long it's been
    since we had anything to celebrate,

since I've done anything
    even *slightly*
    amazing.

Fantastic! Thanks!

Mum puts down her phone.
I got the job!

I look up from mine.
What job?

The job of working evenings
as a market-research
something-or-other
& being paid
slightly less
than the living wage.

Now, while the
twins are sleeping,
she cracks on –

& I creep out,
unnoticed.

CHOICES

It's Saturday, it's hot

& I'm knackered from a morning
      spent on the scorching track:
now I'm happy to be just
      chilling in the trap
      with my fam.

The air inside is warm & thick.
K1's counting a stack of Ps,
      Ben's on his phone,
      Travis is rolling a joint,
      I've just made the coffees.

Rocko's lying in the corner, as usual.

The Viking Line starts buzzing
& K1 flicks a finger at me.
      Get it, bro.
He carries on the count,
      his silent prayer.

                              I hit the button.
            Yo, Viking, yeah, what you want?
                        Yeah . . . Yeah . . .
                    One for three . . . yeah.
                    Three for four . . . OK.

                                    Here?
                  I look at K1 & he nods,
      so I say, *Yeah, come to the yard, man.*
                        You know where.

The TV's on, but no one's watching.
Visitors with cash
      are welcome anytime.

K1's phone plays 2pac

& he steps into the kitchen,
  kicking the door shut
  behind him.

His voice is muffled
  like a silenced shot.
Sounds like bad news.

Oh, f— Yeah, no, chrissakes . . .
He can . . . no . . . no good, he . . .
yeah, I know, it's bitchin' . . .

I look to Travis & Ben
but I can't read their faces.

I take a gulp of too-hot coffee
  & spit it out
  to decorate the table.

What d'ya done, man? Travis asks.

Ain't what he's done,
  says K1,
stepping back in
  & pointing at me.
It's what our brother's
  GONNA do, innit?

He smiles at me,
his gold tooth gleaming
  like a promise.

Turns out, a K1 younger

was supposed to be doing a run
    to the coast, but he
    just vanished off the road.

*Must've got a better offer
    or something*, K1 says,
a black line scowling
    up his frown.

That's why he's looking at me.

We've got a problem, he says.
A problem
    in the shape of
    feeding hungry seaside cats.

But it's one thing
    weeding my own turf
& another crossing the line,
    going country.

I want to tell him I can't just take
    a little trip to the beach:
some of us have got
    commitments.

I've got stuff going on,
like running in the Districts,
like Year Nine's very own
    seaside holiday.

I want to tell K1
    I want to have fun instead,

but I don't even know
    if *no* is an option
    any more.

K1 reads my face

like a road map.

He sits down on the sofa,
    too close.

Look, kid,
    someone's gotta do it.
We look out for each other,
    remember? We're family.

                                   I check out my cousins.

Ben smiles at me, a shifty
    smile that doesn't
    make the shift up
    to his eyes.

                                     Can't they – ?

No! says K1. *Your turn.*
You think you're too good
    to go country?

He leans in &
I can see tiny flakes of scalp
    under the red.
I can smell the coffee
    on his words:
Just do it, Posh Boy.

K1 reaches for the

money on the table
& skims a stack of paper off the top,
    about a centimetre thick.

This is how it is.
Feel this.

He pushes it across &
closes my hand around it.

                    The plastic paper
                        feels warm
                        with welcome.

Good, yeah?
K1 bundles it with a band,
    grabs a Sharpie
    & scrawls ERICK in red
    across a tenner.

You get this
    when you've sold it all,
    when you come back
    with what you owe me.

                  I'm tempted, but . . .
            If it's so easy, why aren't
Ben & Travis biting off his arm?
         Could I have some time
               to think about it?
                     I say.

He pats my shoulder.
    Sure. Gotta take a piss.
& heads off to the toxic bathroom,

                  which gives me all of
                      a minute.

Maybe it's because

Ben & Travis don't want to do it

but still
try to sell it so hard –

C'mon, bro – are you **nuts***?*

K1's gonna have a beef if you don't . . .
Look at the Ps, man!

Or maybe it's because
my heart's doing a
boom-boomity-boom thing,
beating a warning
under my new
Adidas vest,

but when K1 comes back,

I take a breath
& tell him –
in a voice so scared
it hides away –

No.

185

You can see

K1's surprised,
cos his grey eyes widen
   & his nostrils flare.

Ben & Travis's mouths
   are open in shock
   like stuck letterboxes.

The big man stands in front of me
   & I want to get up
   but he's left me no room
   to move.

For a smart boy,
   you just made a
   very stupid decision,
he says slowly,
   & scoops the
   stack of notes into his palm.

The temperature inside the room
   has plummeted
   right down to zero.

Just then

comes the scratch of
   a key in the lock
   & Chantelle's voice calling,
Hi! Anybody home?

She appears in the living room,
   arms wrapped tight round an Asda bag,

& breaks the tension
    like a pencil pops a bubble.

K1 backs off from the sofa
    & I let out the breath
    I've been holding.

I'll pretend you didn't say that,
    Posh Boy, he says.
I'll see you back here
    tomorrow night.

I'm gone so fast
I almost run out of the flat.

I need to think.

I'm starting to feel . . .

    trapped.
trapped.   trapped.
    trapped.

All the long walk home

I'm *thinking, thinking, thinking.*

Normally it's just
    a ten-minute walk
but that's when I'm not
    draaaaagging my heels &
    biting the insides of my cheeks
      to ulcers.

All along the paths of the estate,
between the concrete slabs
    & dumpster bins,
I'm thinking:

> *Is this really the way*
> *I want to go?*

Little kids are shouting,
bouncing a ball
    against the sign
    NO BALL GAMES
& I'm thinking:

> *I shouldn't do this.*

Bigger kids, kids my age,
are hanging outside
    the local shop-in-a-cage,
downing Fanta & crisps,
trackies slung as low
    as their life chances
& I'm thinking:

> *I got other stuff going on.*

Over by the launderette,
Nathan holds the door
    for a woman who might be
    his mother.
His signature Air Max
    are like flowers on his feet,
& I'm thinking:

> *The North Street lot*
> *won't like us moving*
> *on their turf.*

Yo, Posh Boy! Nathan calls,
& I salute him with my fist
as I'm walking, thinking, walking, thinking:

> *I'm so scared to do this,*
> *but then again –*

> I'm shit-scared
> not to.

When I get home

Mum's in a
             right
                   mood –

I can tell from the way she's
    frowning at her phone
& doesn't even say hello.

So I head out for a run
before she can give me
    something else to do.

The rhythm of running
    will help to clear my head.

The running rhythm is

Huh-huh-huh
Bom-bom-bom
Tak-tak-tak

Listen to
   the drums
     of lungs
       & heart
        & feet
       up Gas Hill
then head towards the park,
eyes stinging with sweat.

                     C'mon, Erik!
                     I tell myself.
             You're a smart boy:
everybody says it's true.

                 Think it through.

whatcha gonna –
   huh-huh-huh
whatcha gonna –
   bom-bom-bom
whatcha gonna –
   tak-tak-tak

C'mon, Erik!
whatcha gonna
     do?

I run & run

& reason it all out.

The further I get
   from the trap house, from
   the sudden chill inside that room,
the more I start to calm.

What's the worst
   K1's gonna do to me
   if I say no?
He's not gonna murk me
   just for this, is he?

He won't have real beef with me.
K1 knows I'm no snitch.

Maybe he'll just tell me
   I can't work for him no more.

I'd miss the money,
   but y'know what they say:

Easy come, easy go.

By this time

I'm halfway round
   the park,
my feet thudding
   between the conker trees,

I've decided.

When I get home
    I'll text K1.
I'll say *NO*
& make him
    believe it.

Like a tailwind
    against my back,
relief pushes me
    up to race pace
    until I'm *flying*.

Back home, the front door crashes

back against the wall,
    driving the handle-dent Mum hates
a little deeper.

I hear her in the kitchen,
    making lots of noise.
Pans crashing.

                              MUM! What's for tea?
                              I'm starving!

Oh, you're going to grace us with
your company tonight?

She's still in a mood then.

                    I unlace my trainers & stretch.
                              What's pissed her off
                                        so bad?

In my room, I get distracted by

a video from Ravi,
hairbrush lip-syncing to
    'Sorry Seems to Be the Hardest Word'.

Ravi & I
    spent all half-term
    kind of sniffing round each other
    like dogs in the park,
friends / not-friends
    not sure.

His video is *gruesome*. It might be
    the worst performance I've seen ever
& it makes me laugh so much
    my belly hurts.

Friends.

I sing him back Adele's 'Hello',
recorded from the other side
    of my bed – (see what I did there?) –

& for a little while
    I'm fourteen,
just
    vibing with my mate,

y'know?

Over chilli beans for tea,

Mum tells me
   she's been offered a promotion.
It's a big step up.
No more mop & bucket,
no more early mornings and late nights:
she'll be comfy in an office
   telling other people
   what to do.

> *So what's the face for, then?*
> *That's good news, right?*

It would be, she says,
& swallows,
   if I could afford the childcare.

She says she's tried
   everywhere, everyone, *everything*
   to make it happen
but she just can't get the £££££££££££££££££££££££££££££££££
   the nursery asks for
   upfront.

> *HOW much?*
> I must have heard her wrong.
> They've got to be joking.
> It's a *nursery* – not The Ritz.

Mum starts to cry.

> In my imagination,
> I lick a thumb & finger
> & count – as quickly as K1 –
> the stack of money
> that's mine for the taking.

Before I can slam the lid shut

on memory,
I see Dad's face again,
    lit by the flashing lights
    outside our house.

He whispers,
Look after your mum for me,
    & I promise
as he wheezes
    & squeezes
    my hand real tight.

I promise, I promise
    as they load him onto a stretcher,
    & I cry.

Come on, Erik,
I tell myself.
It's time to
    grow up.

It's time to
    grow up –

        step up –

           be a man.

So, if you're thinking

I'm about to make
   another stupid, selfish, choice,
   you're wrong.

This wasn't selfish.

& it wasn't a choice,
      not really.

PREPARATION

Sunday lunch in the trap house

Chantelle is in the kitchen
   stirring a Pot Noodle.

When K1 hands me the pack
   in a large, grey Nike bag,
he keeps his voice down low.
This is a LOTTA food.
You don't let this bag
   out of your sight,
   you get me?

                                        Yeah, I nod.

Don't trust no one.
And watch out for the North Street lot.
They're worse than the feds.

                                        Copy that.
                                        (Wish I didn't.)

I want your arms wrapped
   round these wraps
   even when you sleep – right?

                                        Right.

& you give the bag to Fritz.
Only Fritz.
Okay?

                                        Okay.
                                        I take the bag
                                        & turn to go.

K1 pats me on the back.
It won't take long
   to clear your pack, Posh Boy –
   those coastal cats are starving.

A few days. That's all.
But the same few days
    I'd planned to spend
    having fun with my mates
    by the sea.

Chantelle comes

running after me,
    heels clattering down the stairs.

Man, you move fast!
I didn't get a chance to say goodbye!
    She smiles.
    She smells like a Lush shop today.
How you doin' anyway, Posh Boy?
Wanna come to the mall
    with me?

Chantelle dangles a shopping bag
    idly from one blue-tipped finger
    as she blocks my path.

                                        Sorry, no – I –
                                    Look, I gotta go.
                            What does she want?

Whassup, Erik? Something wrong?

                                    No, nothing's wrong.
                                    Can I dodge past her
                                    without being rude?

199

She catches my arm
& looks hard at my face
    like she left something there.
You sure?

Between their thick black lashes
    Chantelle's eyes are the
    exact grey-blue
    of Blu Tack.

She lets me go.
    Whatever.
    Look bro, you wanna be
    careful of K1, you know that?

                        Yeah,
                    I call back
          as I race outta there –
                Yeah, I know.
      Soon as this deal's done,
           I'm gonna be
           so careful of K1
        we'll be like strangers.

        I'm getting myself out
              of that trap.

All the way back

I'm saying to myself,
    Just act natural,
but I'm bricking it so bad.

At the sound of every circling
    siren, I'm think I'm gonna faint.

My rucksack's sticking
     to my back already.

For comfort I count
     my footsteps home . . .
Two hundred & forty-five
two hundred & fifty . . .

This is mad.
I've carried lots of weed before
& never been
     so scared.

What's so different now?
Five hundred & fif—

I know what's different.
Five thousand worth of pure Class As
& seven years
     inside.

When I get in

Mum's still grieving
     over the job spec,
trying to balance the books
with a twin tipped
     over her shoulder.

                                   Just going to do some homework!

Thought you said
you'd done it?

Er, no.
Forgot I had to solve
some . . . simultaneous equations.
I pound up the stairs
before she can pick up
there's a new weight
on my shoulders.

& anyway, I do have a problem
    to figure out:

How to be in two
    places
    at the same time.

How to be in two
    places
at the same time.

This is crazy.

I'm off to the seaside
    for the funds to get free,

while the Hardship Fund
    is paying for me

to be by the side
    of a different sea.

Mad.

I'm being picked up

on Tuesday morning,

which is also
    when we leave for
    the Isle of Wight.

Monday's dawn
    starts occurring
    at 03:57 *precisely*.

I know because
    I'm awake for
    the first birds
    cranking it up
    though the crack
    of my window.

They're tweeting
    sleep-sleep
        sleep-sleep
    sleep-sleep
like a scratched vinyl.

But I can't sleep
    because I haven't yet
    figured out a plan

& time is running out.

Monday morning break

It's hot on the field.
The grass is parched to straw.

All the gas today is on
    tomorrow's trip.
My mates can't wait –
they're buzzing with excitement
    like wasps around a doughnut.

At home, my mum has
    packed my rucksack
    already. It's lying
    on my bedroom floor,
straining at the seams.

Me? I've finally
    come up with a plan
    & stuffed it into
    my bulging blazer.

A plan so bold, so barefaced,
    it might just work.

On the field, I protect
    the chipmunk cheek of my pocket
    as carefully as
a face swollen with mumps.

Ravi's super stoked.

He's never even been
　　in a boat before,
　　he says.

He wishes Betty
　　could come too,
　　he says.

He hums the first few bars
　　of 'Sailing',
　　& my throat
　　actually aches.

　　　　　　　　　　　I have to stop myself
　　　　　　　from telling him the truth:

　　　　　　　　　　　Ravi, I really wish
　　　　　　　　　　　　I was going
　　　　　　　　　　　　　　too.

Mr Robinson passes by,

his incredible hulk
　　almost hidden by a
　　huge net bag of footballs.

He spots me, bellows,
OFF ON THE TRIP TOMORROW?

　　　　　　　　　　　　　　I nod –
　　　　　　　　which is not exactly
　　　　　　　　a lie. I *am* going,
　　　　　　　　　　just not on the
　　　　　　　　　　trip he means.

HAVE FUN! he shouts,
   BUT MAKE SURE
   YOU KEEP UP THE RUNNING!
THE DISTRICTS ARE
   SO CLOSE NOW!

I nod again.
You got it, Mr R!

No word of a lie:

I'll be running.

The klaxon sounds

to tell us we've got three minutes
   to get our asses into the Great Hall
   for Monday assembly.

The smokers stub their cigarettes
   out on their boots, stuff mints
   in their mouths

& we all start trooping in.
I let myself drop behind,
   away from Ravi & the rest.

Ravi looks back at me
   & I motion him onward,
   faking a trip to the loo.

I don't want any ricochet, no
   nasty collateral damage.

On either side

of the doorway into the Great Hall,
    two teachers always stand

    guarding the room
    like it was Primark.

Today it's the turn of
    the dynamic duo of
    Mrs Raynor & Monsieur Lebron.

                    Go easy, Erik! I tell myself.
            I need to set this up just right:
                  a *soupçon* too much
             & I'll find myself expelled –

which isn't
    what I'm after
    at all.

Morning, Erik!

says Mrs Raynor, with her brightest
    nice-teacher smile.
Go on in quick – you're late!

Hold on! Monsieur Lebron
    sticks out his hand
    like a traffic cop.
Where's your tie?

In my pocket, I tell him.

In my pocket, SIR! he says.
Put it on, then.

No way, I say. *It's too hot.
Anyway, you're not wearing one.*

The teachers exchange glances.

C'mon, Erik, says Mrs Raynor,
    her smile slipping down from her eyes.
Don't be awkward.

I'm not being awkward, I say,
    *I'm being too hot!
It's like a sodding steam room in there!*

Le Traffic Cop breathes hard
    & goes to grab his handcuffs
    but Mrs Raynor gets in first –
*Less of that, young Erik.
Just go on in & behave yourself.*

She pushes open the door
    & points for me
    to stand at the back.

I slouch back against the wall
    & slip my hands inside my pockets
    (very, very carefully).

So far, so good.
It really *is* roasting in there –
    but still, it's time
    to turn up the heat.

On the podium

Mr Nelson glances up
    from reading out the notices
& glares at whoever's been so bold
    to walk in late – i.e. me.

And finally, he says,
    looking round the hall
    without a smile,
I'd like to wish Year Nine a pleasant trip.
I'm quite sure
    that they'll profit from it
    & that their behaviour at ALL TIMES –
here he pauses
    to look meaningfully
    at me again
    – will be a credit to the school.

Here goes.
My fist closes gently round
    the ammo in my pocket.

I hurl my missiles –

One! Two! Three!

to whizz harmlessly over
    Mr Nelson's head

and splat deliciously
    against the freshly painted scenery
    of the end-of-term play.

I didn't miss.

I'm a good shot.

If I'd *wanted* to hit him,
    I would have.

In the split second of

shocked silence that follows,
    a yellow trail of yolk
              slips
              like
              snot
              off
                    Juliet's balcony.

Then Mr Nelson shouts
    Stop that! &
    the hall detonates into noise.

Teachers yell for quiet
    & the kids just yell,
    craning their necks, trying to see
    who's the crack shot at the back.

Monsieur Lebron dashes in.
He's in no doubt:
    he knows who it was.

He goes straight to where
    I'm stood laughing
    & puts his face
    up close to mine.

ERIK ANDERSEN! he hisses.
This time you've really gone too far!

I shrug
& follow him out the door,
ignoring the whistles
& the teacher's shouts to
Settle down!

I'm hoping that I've gone
just far enough
for what I need.

Result!

I get banned from the trip
with a side order
of a week's suspension –

so exactly what I wanted
that it's hard not to smirk
when they tell me.

I wish I hadn't had to do this,
but even if I say it myself,
I've done it *very well.*

When they try to call my mum

to come & get me,
they can't get through: it
    seems the number doesn't work,
surprise, surprise.

I'm stacking up
    racking up
    jacking up
        my life on
                lies
                lies
                lies
                lies
                lies
                lies
                lies
                lies
                lies
                lies
                lies
                lies.

When the tower topples
it's gonna be absolute *carnage.*

It's like

when people get the sack &
    they have to do the
    cardboard-box security-guard
    walk of shame.

I'm escorted to my locker,
    where there's a toe-tapping wait
    while I take my time hesitating
    over a half-empty bottle of Coke.

Then the welfare officer
    shepherds me out of the gate
in case I'd want to sneak back in
    & stay behind –
    As if.

It's break time &
    I get a lot of stares.

Ravi's with the gang from 9M,
    thumbs tap-dancing on their phones.

My inside pocket's
    buzzing like a bastard
but I'll deal with them –
I'll deal with everyone –
I'll deal with *everything* –
    later,

when I've finished dealing.

At 7 p.m.

we're eating the spaghetti,
   the special goodbye treat.

The twins are smearing
   first-time pureed pasta
   round their mouths,
   loud with joy.

I try to twist spaghetti round my fork
   but my stomach's already
   full of knots; I feel too
   sick to eat.

Face down on the table,
   my phone buzzes, as
   annoying as a fly
   against a window.

We all ignore it.

THE SEASIDE

I don't know the man

in the Audi
    that stops by the chip shop
    at 9:15 a.m.
    precisely.

K1 texted
    DON'T BE LATE

but I had to leave home
    at the usual time,
so I've been hiding
    behind these stinky bins
    for half an hour.

The driver's got a beard
    and a scuffed leather jacket.

Get in.
He hardly looks at me.

Inside, pine air freshener fights
    the fug of weed –
    & loses.

                            I hesitate.
               Do I put my rucksack in the boot?

The driver doesn't move.
He clocks the bag.
You think you're goin' fuckin' camping?

                        Long story, I mutter,
        & wrestle the rucksack along the back seat
               where it lies the whole journey
                  like a sleeping passenger.
                         Or a corpse.

I hunker down

& pull my cap over my eyes,
    until we hit the ring road
& we're speeding east
    towards the coast.

Buildings flatten
    out to fields:
        high hedges   hem
               the   road
              like   bumpers
               on   a
       bowling   lane.

This is it: I'm really
    going country.

This is it.

I clutch the backpack tightly to my chest
wishing my heart
    wasn't jumping to meet it.

I'm playing K1's words
    like they're on repeat:
Don't let that bag
    out of your sight, Posh Boy –
& don't trust no one.
Not no one. Not ever.

The driver doesn't

speak again.

He just drives.

One hand on the wheel,
    the other chain-smoking
    in little puff-puff-puffs,

tapping the ash
    off the edge of the window
    between each one

       puff
              tap
       puff
              tap
       puff
              tap,

sunlight glinting off
    his big gold rings.

> After a while, the silence
>   gets kinda awkward,
> so I cough to clear my throat
>   & ask,
> *Where we goin' then?*

But he doesn't answer.

> Has he heard? I try again.
> *Where's it at then?*

This time
he turns his head & says,
You'll soon find out.

Then he touches the dash
& starts nodding to Frosty,
& I keep my head still,
& just stare
    out the window,
my guts beginning to churn.

What am I doing here?

The telegraph poles
    whip past. I count them
one-two-three-four . . .
one-two-three-four . . .
But the spell isn't working now.

I wish I'd gone to the
    bathroom before I left
    but I didn't,

& I don't think
    my driver's gonna stop
    for my convenience.

Fields.

Cows. A barn with a massive banner:

> ## *WEDDING RECEPTIONS!*
> ## *BIRTHDAY & ANNIVERSARY PARTIES!*

Anniversary . . . anniversary . . .

That word's like a crowbar
    prising open my Dad-box.
This year would've been
    my parents' crystal wedding.
Fifteen years.

Just before the pandemic,
Dad put a finger to his lips
    & led me up the garden to
    our rickety wooden shed.
Shhh!

Inside, hidden under stacks of
    cobwebby clay pots,
    there it was –
an old biscuit tin with
    Dad's squiggly writing:

    Anniversary Holiday Fund

He opened it with a showbiz *Ta-da!*
Queen Liz stared sadly up at me
    from a single, solitary, fiver.

I blinked. Dad laughed.
Gotta start somewhere!

> We're past the barn now.
> I jam the lid back on,
>   tighter.

While the miles go by

I go back to figuring out how in hell
I'm gonna slip my mum
        the money for the nursery:
no paper round
        pays this kinda paper,
        does it?

What can I say?

Hey, look what I found! A coupla grand
Just lying in the street! Fancy that!

Yeah, right.

How can I make it legit?
        How can I wash that dirty money
        clean with lies?

How can I wash it
        so clean
        we can *eat* off it?

An hour later

we draw up to some lights
        by a harbour wall
& I can see the sea.

Memory grabs me
        like a hand around
        my ankle, tripping me up.

I'm a teenie – just ten or so,
Dad in the driving seat,
Mum singing out,
Who can see the sea?
Who can see the sea?

I can! I can!
I can! I can!

The beach.

Dad holding my hand tight
    in the crowds.
Wind. The crunch of pebbles.
The promise of an ice cream
    if I'm good.

I want to play on
    every single game in
    every single arcade
    right along the pier –

& I do.

Dad takes me,
& I lose (I remember exactly)
a grand total of £10.75
    & it's *amazing*,

right up till we get chips,
    when I'm bombed by a massive seagull
        with a beak like a pirate's sword
    & I cry & I cry & I cry.

Then I'm safe again
    in the warm nest of his T-shirt,
Dad's hand cupping my head as
    he soothes me,
Vær modig, min liten viking, vær modig.

Now I breathe
   the weed in deep
to stop the freak
   from fighting its way out.

Vær modig.
Vær modig.
Vær modig . . .
Be brave.

Be brave, my little Viking.

The lights change.

We turn left

away from the sea & the slot machines,
away from the pier
   & the pubs
   & the promenade,

& crawl through the back streets of B&Bs,
   & the peeling paintwork
   & the *ROOMS AVAILABLE.*

The driver makes a call:
Hey, Fritz?
Bringing him now. Yeah. Erik.
     . . . . *Nah, we're here. Now. Yeah.*

We turn again & the car draws up
  outside a narrow house, its
  cracked door dirty white,
the front garden growing
  gravel & beer cans & bin bags,
the windows blanked off with
  faded Mickey Mouse
  wrapping paper.

The driver switches off the music
& then there's only the soft *tick-tick*
  of the engine
rapping with the hard beat
  of my heart.

Welcome to your new home!

says my driver,
  widening his mouth
  to flash a missing tooth.

When I don't move, he adds,
  What, you waitin' for someone
  to invite you in, is it?

           I shake my head.

So get out & get sellin' the food!
  he says, slamming a hand
  on my rucksack.
K1 ain't payin' you
  to sit on your arse
  in my car.

I get out slowly, my
legs stiff & my intestines
cramping like a twisting snake
cos I really need the loo.
Aren't you coming in?

I'm just the driver, he says,
flicking a butt
like a tiddlywink
onto the pavement.
*Your new housemates
are waitin' for you.
Go say hello.*

He spits out of the window
& drives away.

I go up

the path & hesitate
by the door,
squeezing my butt cheeks together.
Knock or ring?

I need the bathroom
so *bad* . . . maybe I can
just walk on in?

But I don't have to, cos
it swings wide
& a lad comes out,
wheeling a bike.

I step back.
Uh, hi.

He looks up at me
with no interest.

He's young – Year Six? Year Seven?
Skinny. A green baseball cap
pulled low over a pinched face.
Scabbed lip. Huge eyes
like a – like a what? –
Like a *tarsier.*

He tells me
Fuck off
like it was *Hello,*

then gets on his bike
& pedals off.

I take a deep breath
& push the door wider.
Hi? Anybody home?

There's no hall.

The front door leads
straight into a narrow room
where the air is thick & funky
with the smell of weed.

It's dim in there, the light
filtered through paper
taped onto the windows.

In the underwater gloom
    I'm blinded after
    the sunlit street.

A deep voice says
Gimme the pack, fam,
& a dark shape
    rises from the sofa,
hands stretched out
    to grab my bag –

                          No! I hug it tighter,
                              remembering K1's
                              Don't trust no one.

As my eyes adjust
    I see a room
messy like it
    just got hit by a tornado.

Broken chairs,
a sofa with the foam
    erupting out,
bottles & cans & takeout cartons,
a coffee table with a bong,
a dirty T-shirt,
a set of scales.

The *smell*.

This place makes the
    Nightingale trap house look like
    it's been keeping up with
    the Kardashians.

The guy who wants my pack

is massive, dressed in
     a running vest & boxers, but
the running vest's too small
     for the big furry belly
     that swells
     underneath it.

He laughs a rumbling laugh.
You're Erik, right? I'm Fritz.
Settle down, my man.
What's the issue?

                                    I need to use
                           your bathroom, that's all,
               I say, looking at the filthy carpet.
                                        No issue.

He holds out his hand again,
& I see a bear claw
     etched in ink
     across its hairy back.

So give, he says,

                                    & this time
                                  (reluctantly)
                                       I do.

I try again.

So, can I use the bathroom?

Fritz growls,
    Upstairs.

If I thought the
    living room was grim,
the bathroom really
    has it beat.

Every
    excretion
        everywhere.

Brown smears down the walls
    that could be dried blood.

Brown smears on the seat
    that probably aren't.

I don't breathe through my nose.
I touch as little as I can
& do what I have to do
in record time.

The sooner I'm out of here,
the better. This place
is a real
shithole.

When I come back down

I'm surprised to see
    a woman in the front room
    stooping to pick up crockery,
her hand a mug tree.

She's not young but
    her dark hair's long & loose –
    like a girl's, except it's streaked
    with grey.

Wanta coffee?
    she asks me,
    in a foreign accent.

                                    I nod *Yes* –
                 then remember the *please*.

This is Maria,
    says Fritz. He's
    back on the sofa,
busy with scales & bags.
Maria's Mikey's mum –
    You must've met him
    coming in.
Mike the Bike,
    says Fritz,
    That's what I call him,
    the little shit.

He laughs again,
a grizzly rumble.

Maria was on her way out of the room,
    eyes glued to the
    sticky carpet,

but now
    she stops & stands by Fritz.
'E's not a shit,
    she says quietly.

She lifts her lowered head
    & looks him in the eye.
    You don't call
    my son a shit.
Not in my own 'ouse.

The flash of a bear paw
    & Maria cries out.
The mugs crash to the floor.

Fritz roars in her face.

IT'S NOT YOUR
FUCKING HOUSE
THOUGH, IS IT?
NOT NOW!

I heard somewhere

that a grizzly bear
    can crush a bowling ball
    with a single swipe.

Maybe Maria was lucky
    she only got
    a bloody nose.

After Maria

runs from the room,

Fritz says,
What you starin' at?
& carries on weighing & cutting,
his big hairy fingers
surprisingly nimble.

He brushes a bit
of broken china
to the floor.

                                        I can't think
                                    of what to say,
                                so I sit beside him,
                        hug my knees to my chest

                                                & say

                                            nothing,

                                        nothing at all.

What was I

expecting?

The comfy, cosy, family feel
    of the Nightingale flat?

This has all the
    cosiness

of a bear pit.

The Viking Line's

busy with orders all day,

but the school always gives orders
    about phones on trips,

so I know I don't have to
    switch on my iPhone
    till 6 p.m.,

when we get a
    measly thirty-minute
    phone ration.

I step outside
    into the tiny back yard,
sit on an upturned crate
    & wait.
At six-oh-three
    it buzzes,
right on cue.

Hi, Mum.

Are you having a good time?

Mum asks.

Yeah.

Doing lots of fun stuff?

Yeah.

Have you been sailing yet?

Yeah.

*Please say something else besides
'yeah'. Was it exciting?*

Yep.

Very funny. So are the dorms nice?

There are two bedrooms:
Fritz has the big one, leaving

Maria & Mikey to
cram onto a single bed
in a room the size of a
shoebox.

I've got a pushbike
but no bed at all –

I'm on the sagging sofa,
which turns out to
have fleas or something.

Scratch. Scratchity. Scratch.

Yeah.

Before I can switch it off,

my iPhone rings again.
It's Ravi. Shouts in the background. Laughter.

Erik! How are you, mate?

                                             Fine.

It's so cool here. We got to sail a boat today!
Adam fell in! Only he didn't fall, he jumped.

                              Of course he did.

We're trying paddleboards tomorrow. Can't wait!

                        Yeah, well, lucky you.

A pause. *Sorry.*

                                           Sorry.

I bet your mum was really mad.

                                           Yeah.

What did she do to you, then?

                    Look, man, I don't really want
                         to talk about it, okay?

Fair.
. . .
So what you doing today?

                    I look at the stash on the table,
                         the baggies full of pills
                  & lumps of rock & green-grey weed.

                                        Nothin'.

Fritz

weighs
   & cuts
      & chops
         & bags
with the speed
   of a fast-food chef.

                 I hold the line
              & take the orders.
We got white, green & brown.
Three for three?
Yeah man, Got that . . .
One for two, two bags.
Gotcha . . . yeah . . . same place,
the pier . . .

Then me & little Mikey
   set off on our bikes,
   pedalling our flavours
   to the starving moggies.

Pretty quick
   we're the busiest
   takeout in town.

The seaside cats

aren't so different
   from the alley cats
   I'm used to.

Maybe there aren't so many
   cool cats

or shiny-coated
   pedigree party animals,

maybe there are a few more
   mangy strays,

but it's true
   what they say –

all cats
   are grey
   in the dark.

I don't think Mikey

likes me.

On that first night,
in the low tides between
   whispers & rustling paper
& knuckle rubs
   from strangers

               I ask him for his story:
               why he's not at school,
               how come he & Maria
               live with Fritz.

Neon lights from the
        arcades bounce across
        his sharp cheekbones

& he stares at me
like I'm a total
        twat.
        We just do, he says.

                                    I open my mouth

but he closes it for me –
Not your business, is it?

He turns his back
& powers down
        the conversation
        like a dying phone.

It's then I spot
        the marks on his
        arms & legs – not flea bites, like mine,
but blistered burns,

& I get it.

Mikey's even more frightened
        than I am.

The hours of sleep

are short here, only
        catnaps grabbed
        between the
        feeding of the cats.

With no bed,
I just tip sideways
   on the lumpy
     bug-infested sofa,

my arms wrapped
   tightly round me
   for a quilt.

I try to be

on my own
   when Mum calls.

Just before six on the third evening,
I say I'll go out for
   chicken wings.

I never thought you could
   get sick of burgers –
but then, I've never eaten burgers for
breakfast, lunch & dinner,
   three days straight.
Turns out, you can.

I open the door
 & stick my head out cautiously, like a meerkat,
   checking for feds
   or the North Street gang.

Fritz says we gotta get outta here
   before they get a fix on us, but
   we're nearly done.

It's all clear.
The evening sun's still
    warming the pavement
    as I head towards the pier.

I've been this way already
    so many times, feels like I know it
    better than the route to school.

I miss Ravi.

I'm so tired.

K1 said,
    Get in. Get rich. Get out.
    Get it?

I start running, counting
    my steps for comfort.
One, two . . .

The promenade is stiff with traffic,
bumper-to-bumper-to-bumper-to-bumper.
The happy holidaymakers
    are heading home.

Mum's ringtone
    stops my count at
    three thousand & thirty-four.

I slow down &
    touch her face.

Hey, Mum.

You sound funny.

Sure you're okay?

> I picture Mum on
> hands-free: blitzing bottles & bums,
> swiping snot.

> *Yeah. Just tired.*
> I lift the corners of my mouth
> to put a smile inside my voice.
> *Howz you?*

We're all right.
The girls are missing their big bro!

Alice – or Esme –
    backs her up
    by bursting into noisy tears.

> *I miss them too,* I say,
> & it's true. I do.

> I miss them all.
> I miss home.

> *I'll see you soon.*

I'm going to have to
    turn the job down, Erik.

> & even over the wailing,
> I can't miss the rip in her voice.

I've tried to borrow, but no one's got
that kind of money
    in their back pocket,
have they?

She doesn't know it, but
she just doesn't know
the right people.

Hang in there, Mum!
Something will turn up,
I know it will.

Just two more days.
Hang on.

By dawn

Fritz is almost smiling.
It's the first time
    he's done anything
    but scowl.

Like we're the only line
    in town! he growls,
holding up a
    bulging zip-bag
    like a football trophy.

I told K1 we didn't need to
    shank no one. We just had to
    feed them cats their
    favourite food,
    innit?

One more night

& we'll have emptied the pack.
   Sold out.

I can go home.
I'll get my money from K1,
   give it to Mum –
& that's it.

It's over.

No more.

I'm *done*.

Halfway through

a final McBreakfast,
   I swallow my coffee
   to answer the Lyca
   one last time for luck.

Yo, Mikey's line!
This cat has gotta
be the last, the
cupboard's almost
bare.
Whatcha after?

YOU,
says a stranger.

I freeze, the
hot mug burning
in my hand.

We already gave K1
  his final warning,
  says the voice.
We told him to get off
  North Street turf.

                A cold blade of fear
                   slices between
                     my ribs.

Now we're gonna
  have to
  kill you.

& just like that,
the line goes
  dead.

TRAPPED

We split so fast

there's hardly time to pack our stuff.

We's all done here anyway.
See you next time.
Don't miss me too much!
says Fritz, reaching out
    his giant paw to Mikey –
    who doesn't shake it.

Suit yerself, Fritz growls.

Maria glares at him,
dragging her son in close
    with a protective arm.
You can just fuck off
    & don't come back!

On the pavement by his car,
    the bear announces
    he's going into hibernation:
The North Street gang,
they know my face now,
    innit?

He opens the door.
Warm plastic-flavoured air guffs out
K1 says I'd better
    lie low for a while.

At least I get a lift to the station.

I've got money for the fare
but the real money's in the pouch
strapped under my T-shirt
like a suicide belt.

You don't open that.
You don't take it off.
You don't give it to no one else
    but K1. Got that?

Got it.
All of it.

Thirteen minutes to go

before my train.
Walking along the platform
    there's nowhere to hide.
My hair doesn't help:
wish I'd worn a cap.

I choose an empty carriage
& slip into a window seat,
wedging my massive rucksack
    in the space beside me
    for camouflage.

Breathe. Breathe.
Count the breaths,
    slow & steady . . .
try to calm my heart.

Was I followed?
Do the North Street crew
    know I'm here?

Through the glass I watch
    a sweating man
    pulling a wheelie case,
a train guard strutting like a cockerel,
two giggling red-shouldered girls
& a mother dabbing ice cream
    from her dress.

Breathe.

No one who
    looks like they've got a knife
    or a beef to settle.

The numbers glowing

on the board
    change
so
    agonisingly
             slowly:
    ten

minutes

        have

      never

    felt

         so

long.

By the time a whistle *PHEEEEEEPS*

sweat's dripping off my face.

The guard's arm drops,
& we shuffle off.

Outside town, the train
picks up speed.
the trackside scrub
        start to blur
& I focus on the chant of the wheels:

I'm going home . I'm going home . I'm going home . . .

This clammy bundle
        soaked with my fear & stuck flat
        to my skin: it was all for this, *this*.

I fold my hands over the money
        as protection, like a defender
        facing a penalty shot.
This is my key to freedom.
This is the ticket out.

I'm going home . I'm going home . I'm going home . . .

The flat land's flashing past.

Behind me, the carriage doors
        hissssssss open
& I hear a hustle of bodies
        clattering through the gap.

A young male voice is shouting,
        I saw him! Nah, he's here, bro,
        fo' sure, it's this one.
I saw him come in here.

& all at once
    I realise how dumb I was,
sitting by myself.
No witnesses.

Of all the bad decisions I've made,
    this could be
    the worst.

I'm actually trapped in my seat

by that stupid rucksack wedged next to me.
The voices are close, so close.

                            I hunker down, head low –

You hidin' from us, my man?
Give it up, boy! We know you're here!

                                    I hold my breath –

Come on outta there!

                            They *must* be able to see me –

Hey! We can see you! Game's up, bro!

                                    They're right behind me –

You ignoring us? We talkin' to you!

                                        I shut my eyes –

Yeah, YOU!

                            & wait for the knife in my guts.

Who, me?!

calls a young voice,
    sweet as a doughnut.

                                        I open my eyes.

A giggling head has
    popped up from the
    – not empty! –
    seat in front.

It's a boy with tight curly hair
    who's laughing so hard
he's got snot
        coming out
           of his nose.
Ha ha, what took you so long?
I thought
    you'd never find me!

He knocks triumphant
    knuckles with his brothers
& they cuff him
    gently round the head.
You run off like that again, Lemmy
& we'll tell Mum,
& she'll kill you, dope!

                            My heart starts to slow.

                            I press myself back
                                into my seat,
                turn my face to the window,
                      & listen to what
                    the train is telling me.
              You fool. You fool. You fool.

I'm gonna change my life.

As of right now.

I can make the train's wheels change their tune:
I can do this. I can do this.
I can do this.
I . can . do . this .
I can.

I can turn it all around.

So I send a single text –

> *On train.*
> *Be there soon.*
> *& I am OUT. No more.*

Then switch off both my phones.

I'm sweating

& panting,
& running the whole half-mile
    from the station
    to the trap house,
to this last ever
    meeting with K1.

That's it. It's *over*.
    I'm getting what I'm owed
    & I'm outta this life.

This rucksack weighs a **ton**,
    but I can't wait
    to get it done,

so I jog the quick way,
    through
    the
    narrow
    alley
    to the estate,

listening to my beats,
counting down the minutes
    to my freedom.

Now I'm in the welcome

shadows of the alley by the Flo,
earbuds pumping out
    Ravi's dadrock,
the *Ha!-Ha! Ha!-Ha!* song
    for learning CPR.

Oh, *yeah* –
    this is me, I'm staying alive,
& I'm singing along,
    blasting it out,
& I'm really not hearing
    what's roaring up the alleyway
    right behind me,

until the hot breath of the motorbike
    is on my heels
    & I look round
    & it's
        too late.

The alley is walled

     left   right,
   there's   nowhere
nowhere   nowhere
nowhere   nowhere
nowhere   nowhere
nowhere   nowhere
   to escape.

The bike cuts past

& knocks me flat.

The back wheel skids a circle

& the pillion
   leaps off,
& leans over me,
   his brightly patterned trainers
   STOMPING footprints on my chest.

I struggle but
   I can't get up –
   I'm flat on my back,
anchored by the weight
   of the rucksack,
   helpless as a turtle.

My own terror's staring
   wide-eyed back at me,
reflected in a
   mirrored visor.

A sickening slice
    of pain as he
    swings back &
    kiiiiiiiiiiiiiicks.

& I'm screaming
    at the sharp glint
    of a blade
    flashing in his hand.

The knife *slashes* up
    & slices –

& my pouch is gone.

There's a laugh,
    one more kick in my ribs,
& the motorcycle's roar
    rips up the alley.

Curled on the ground
    I'm gasping with shock,
    listening to the sound of the engine
    fade away, & with it
    my hopes of freedom.

When I can breathe again,
    I clamber to my feet
& hobble into the
    high-rise hell
    of the Nightingale Estate.

I don't know how to tell him,

but my silence says it all.

K1's eyes are granite
    looking at the
    ribbon of blood
    streaking the cut T-shirt,

gaping open to show
    only a slice in my skin
    where his money
    should be.

Lying on the floor

of the Nightingale trap,
I'm curled like a woodlouse
    trying
        in vain
            to protect
        my soft
   middle.

K1 aims careful kicks
until my body
        exPLOdes with pain.

You're not – (kick) – OUT!
until I say you're – (kick) – OUT!

                       I wrap my arms around my head
                               & pray
                         to pass out.

So this is it?

It's all been
    for nothing?

A great big, fat zer**O** ?
Fritz, the lies
    the fear, the *fleas*
      Mikey, Maria, *everything* . . . ?

All of it?

All for nothing?

I can't bear it.

Gradually, the tempo . . .

    of the blows . . .

    slows . . .

like maybe K1's
    getting bored.

Breathing like a boy trapped in a locker

because it hurts so much,
I look for my voice
where it has
hidden
inside
me,
&
ask
K1 for
what is
rightly mine,
for what I earned,
for what I've paid for
twice, in fear & pain & blood . . .

But what about the money? My money? My money? My money?

I open my eyes.

K1's mouth is twisted with surprise:
his scar rears like a rattlesnake
    up his cheek.
You just lost me
    twenty grand!

He aims a final
    slap at my head
but it's lame,
like I'm not even worth
    beating up
    any more.
I'll say this for you, kid.
You've got guts.

                  Please, I whisper
               through swollen lips.
        Please can I have that money?
              You promised . . .
                  I NEED it.

Instead of kicking me again

K1 steps back &
   folds his arms across his chest.
What d'you need it for it so bad, man?

                  & it spills out of me like
                  the torrent from my nose.

                        I tell him
            all about Alice & Esme,
              all about Mum's job,
             all about Dad dying.

                 Tears & blood
           leak into my words like
             punctuation marks.

When I dribble to a halt
   there's a silence.
The tap   d d
             r   r
             i   i
             p p
                s
            in the kitchen.

Tell me you still got the burner, man.

                      It's safe,
            deep in my rucksack.

                        I nod.

K1 sighs.
Shrugs.
Reaches into
    his pocket.
You're looking after your fam.

He peels
    the papers from his fold
like he's dealing me a hand.

Call me a fool,
    he says,
tucking the rest of his wad out of sight,
    but I like you.
    I'm gonna see you right.

He holds out the money,
    but as I reach for it
his other hand
    circles my wrist.
    like a handcuff.
This is a gift from me, bro.
*A **gift**. Get that?*

His voice is cold as metal.

But you owe me now.
Don't you ever –
    NEVER –
    forget it.

He lets me go.
Now get your face
    cleaned up.
Whatever is your mother
    going to think?

In Rocko's filthy bathroom

> I change my clothes.
> I rip my bloodied T-shirt into strips,
> dab it at my swelling lips.

Over the sound of the running water
K1's voice calls –
>> *Erik! Come out here.*
>> *Our conversation. I've been thinking . . .*

He's got a
>> square-shaped
>> something in
>> his hands: a
>> black-wrapped
>> dictionary-sized
>> mummy of
>> gaffer tape.

Erik, my man . . .
He puts the package
>> in my hands.

> It's a lot of gear.
> Must be a kilo, easy.

Keep this for me,
>> he says.

> It's too much.
> If the feds found it
> I'd be inside for years.

For the weekend,
      he says.
I gotta go on the road,
      he says.
I don't trust Rocko or Chantelle
      to keep their thieving mitts
      off of my grub, you copy?

                              Just for the weekend? That's all?

I tell you what, Erik,
he says,
& puts his face up close to mine
      until his shark-grey eyes
      are all I see.

Make it good between us.
Do me this last favour & we'll be quits.
You can walk away.

Put it somewhere very safe.
Don't open it.

I'm trusting you, he says,
      not to fuck up.

                                          Too late.
                                          I already did.

Leaving the trap house

I go the long way back
    to avoid the alleyway,
scuffing my heels
    through the long slanting shadows of the Flo.

A bunch of teenies are yelling,
    throwing themselves into freefall
    from the swings. Having fun.

The air smells warm, of dandelion & dogshit.
I remember being that happy.

It's hot. Everything hurts.
But at least I've got the money.
I'll figure out the rest later.

My iPhone buzzes.

    When are you getting back?
    I miss you!
    The girls too.

Mum.
She's going to be so happy
    to see me . . .

I check my face in my phone.
Blood is drying into dark
    crusts on the cuts
    on my clownish lips.
A bruise is already starting to stain
    my cheekbone blue.

. . . or perhaps
    she won't.

On my phone

there's a message from Chantelle
   I missed before.

      BE CAREFUL!

Too late.

Beyond the swings,

by the old gardener's hut,
   Nathan is doing a deal.

Even from here,
   the bright butterfly wings
   of his signature Air Max
   stand out.

He looks my way & slowly
   raises a middle finger.

The penny drops
   (too late) –

I'm the mug
   who just got mugged
   twice over.

One look at my face

& Mum goes *mental* –

wielding wads of cotton wool like scouring pads,
firing accusations of abuse like bullets,
roasting the school roundly.

> *Chill, Mum! It looks worse than it feels.*
> *They said they'd emailed you . . .*
> *I just got bashed by an oar,*
> *that's all.*

I can see her thinking, *Bashed by an oar? How many times?*
But then a baby sister starts to wail
& it's teatime & she gives it up
& finally hugs me a hello

> & I smile, while
> I really
> want to cry.

I'm tunnelling

deep in the heap
    at the bottom of my cupboard,

looking for someplace
    to stash the stash where
    no one's gonna poke their nose.

I ditch my ancient collection
    of dehydrated felt-tips
& put the package in their place,
    hiding the tin back
    under a sediment of crap.

At teatime

I'm back on my throne:
the homecoming king
        flanked by his high-chaired courtiers.

                        I put my face close to Alice's
                        & go *BOO!* to make her laugh.

She giggles & pokes a finger at
        the black of my eye,
the scarlet of my split lip:
her mouth makes an O of wonder that a
        brother can come in these colours.

Mum ladles lasagne onto my plate

                                                &
                I shovel it in like I'm mixing concrete.
        After four days of fast food, it tastes so *goooooooood.*

                        Everything is good.
                This is us, this is us *turning the corner.*

                I'll find a way to give her the money.
                        Mum'll take the new job.
                        Life'll get back to normal.

Mum squints at my face & tuts
        like she does
        when she sees the state of my bedroom.
Are you okay to race on Monday?

                                        I choke.
                                        I forgot!
                        I *totally* forgot the Districts.

Two days?

I can do it.
I can.

I'm the King of Teatime,
I'm the ruler of the Holland Road Track Team.

> I crack a smile that smarts.
> *I don't race with my face, do I?*
> I'm so glad she can't see
> the boot-shaped bruises.
> stomped across my ribs.

Mum puts out a hand & rubs my knuckles
    warm with love.
Brave lad. Your dad would be so proud,
if he knew.

> & I'm so glad
> he doesn't.

Just before sleep

steals me away,
I make the connection . . .

Dad. Tins. Hidden things.
I know how I can get Mum
    to accept the money.

I'm a *genius*.

TREASURE

At sunrise

my alarm softly *peep-peeps.*

Everything hurts.
It feels like I've hardly been asleep,
but on the wall by my nose
   my training schedule's
   pinned up like a question:

Am I in good enough shape to run?

YES.

I am.
I will be.
I have to be.
K1's not gonna stop me.

I swing my legs out of bed
& bite back a swear
   at the pain.
C'mon, Erik!
You got this.

But first . . .
   there's something more important
   I gotta do.

I tiptoe through the house

so as not to wake the girls
& give the game away.

The grass is long & cold & wet
    around my ankles.
The flat roof of the shed steams gently.
It's gonna be a hot one.

The grassy warmth inside the shed
    feels like going back in time:

Dad's bike's still on its back,
    begging for attention.

Mud, grey & dry, is
    crumbling off spades & forks.

There's the old smell of dust & turpentine.

I don't think I've even opened the door since –
                      since –
                      since –

Memories start
    filtering in like the sunlight
    fighting through the filmy window.

                                                Dad.

I have to stop for a moment.

Breeeeeeeeathe. Let him in.

                    Dad, I'm sorry I messed up.
                          I'm making it right,
                              I promise.

I remember where to look:

under a towering pile of terracotta pots,
    blanketed in cobwebs.

Layers of clay grind against each other
    as I find it, still safely
    tucked underneath.

A rusted tin with a still-legible label.
    Anniversary Holiday Fund
Seeing Dad's handwriting
    makes me swallow hard.

                           Don't think too much.

I lever it open, empty my pockets
    & give the lonely Queen
    a lot of company.

Mum's gonna get such a surprise today
    when I offer to cut
    the grass.

Oh, Erik!

Mum comes running crossly to the shed
    when she hears the crash of falling pots
as I clumsily drag out the mower.

What's this? she asks,
    pointing at the tin,
swiping at a trailing piece of cobweb
    in her hair.

I pretend to peer at it, & shrug.
Dunno.

She looks closer.
It's . . . It's Dad's writing.

She reads,
& her voice trembles
What the . . . ?

Open it, Mum!

She does.

Later, after mum stops crying

– & she cries a *lot,*
tears dripping on the keyboard
as she types at thirty words a minute,
    yes! to the nursery,
    yes! to the job –

we make a list
& she goes shopping
    while I mind my sisters.

Alice & Esme & me
    are sitting on the kitchen floor
    with my old toy cars

when Mum come back with
    her arms full of bags of amazing food,
stuff we haven't had since Dad died.

I can't believe
she managed to get it all home
on the bus.

I put it all away for her.
(though some of it gets
put away in me.)

mangoes
blueberries
chicken breast, fat steaks
big prawns
proper fish fingers
Prosecco x 2
huge bag of crisps
posh hot chocolate
Coca-Cola x 2
sushi
Peperamis
bubble bath
Eco nappies
Ben & Jerry's
massive chocolate cake
luxury loo roll
fresh herbs
asparagus
free-range chicken
real exotic juice

CAR CRASH

But that's when

it all starts to go wrong.

I saw Mr Choudhri
    in the shop, Mum says, her face still red from
    happiness, heat & hauling the bags.

Alice grizzles & Mum
    gallops her up [&] down on an ankle.

I told him the good news!
He said Ravi would love
    to come & celebrate
    with us tomorrow night.

                                    That's great! I lie.
                                    It's not great.
                                    It's a *disaster.*

Ravi. Who thinks
    I spent last week with Mum.

Mum. Who thinks
    I spent last week with Ravi.

Esme smacks her toy bus into Alice
    & Alice screams.

This is gonna be an absolute *car crash.*

This can't happen.

Ravi's got his invite.

He phones me.
He's thrilled, of course he is:
Prawn curry,
    chocolate cake
& a side order of babies . . .
What's not to like?

He doesn't get my hints that he's not welcome.

I've missed you, man!
he says, all excited.

                      I can hear
                Simon & Garfunkel
      playing on his dad's old deck.

I've got so much
    to tell you 'bout the trip –

                      – Yeah, I cut in.
                    About the trip. Look.
                  Do me a big one, bro?
        Make like I was there with you all week.
                Will you do that for me?

                      I wait.

But from Ravi's end,
there's nothing.

Just the
    sound of silence.

279

Then he explodes.

I haven't seen him this mad since
     Covid cancelled Costello.

We argue on the phone
     for ages as he
     tugs & pulls & worries out the truth,
shred by painful shred.

                    I turn Alice's teddy bear over in my hands,
                              slowly picking out
                         the stuffing through a hole.

I can't believe I defended you to Betty!
Ravi's voice is coming out
     in a Year Seven squeak.
She said *you were mixed up with drugs!*
She said *she'd seen you at the Flo!*

I think he might be actually crying.
I'm swallowing hard myself.

I told Betty you'd never do that.
I told her you'd never be so stupid!
How COULD you?

What's the point of trying to be friends with you?
I don't mean a thing to you!
This
     just
          proves
                    it.

                         I don't get a chance to explain
                              before he cuts the call
                         & the teddy bear's left hanging
                              limply from my hand,
                              as empty as I feel.

I lost my best friend

I just . . . threw him away.

I pull on some shorts,
plug in some tunes
& run, run, run,
    as fast as I can.

Ignoring the pain from my kicking,
I sweat my way around Lion Wood &
    through the cemetery,
swerving Dad's grave as per usual.

                    thud-thud-thudding
                    thud-thud-thudding
                    thud-thud-thudding

Around the front of the church,
evening bells tolling the time
    right through my earbuds.

                      running away
                      running away
                      running away

Out onto the straight road,
running west with the wind from the sea.

                      one-two-three
                      one-two-three
                      one-two-three

beating myself up to a rhythm
like the heart-blood in my ears.

Halfway up Gas Hill,

I'm done.
I can't go any further.

I lean on a white-barked tree
& try to whoop some air back
   to my aching lungs.

Every breath
   is like a knife
   running along my ribcage.

How did I do?
I'm checking my time
   when a text from Chantelle
   lands on my screen, like a note
   wrapped around a stone.

> *did u hear?*
> *mikey got shanked.*
> *in his leg. he's in hosp.*
> *north st says they done it.*

Shock stabs through me like the
   blade through Mikey's thigh.

Little Mikey.
So scared & scarred.

It's not fair!
Mikey's just a teenie, a tiddler –
too small to be trapped in the net.

It's Fritz they should have fished for.

I hang onto the tree
   as Mum's treats
   surf up out of my guts,
riding a wave of guilt.

Next morning,

smells of spices &
    the sound of singing
    rise up through the house
& trickle under my door.

Mum's cooking early.
She says you gotta let a curry
    settle in,
    like a new cat.

She sounds so happy.

How can I tell her Ravi's not coming?
How can I tell her he hates me?

How can I tell her –
can I ever tell her? –
how much I hate myself
    right now?

Plans change.

A message from K1 comes in
    as soon as I switch out from 'sleep' mode:

      FRITZ NEEDS THAT PACK URGENT.
      TAKE IT TOMORROW. DON'T OPEN IT.

                    Adrenaline kicks me
                    fully awake in seconds.
                    Tomorrow?
            That's the day of the Districts!

                        How abt Tues?

                        Please, please.

K1 shoots back
    straight from the hip:

    TOMORROW. DO IT.

I'd like to ask him how Mikey is
but I don't really think
    he cares.

The more I think about it

the more I understand
   why they use youngers.

It's not a career path.
We're not being groomed
   for stardom.

We're dispensable.
We're cannon fodder.
K1 is sending me
   over the top, deep
   into enemy territory.

I'm crossing the

        l
        i
         n
        e
            again.

There's a giggle & a scuffle

outside my door
& the soft tap-tap tap-tap-tap tap-tap
of Mum's special knock
    for when I've done no wrong.

                I open the door
                   just a crack.
                     Yes?

Mum wants me to look after Esme.
Alice is sleeping,
    & she's got stuff to do.
Can you?

                       If I must.
        I take the warm bundle of wriggle
              & blow *hello* on her tum.

Esme laughs.

             I imagine her when she's older,
      standing hand in hand with her sister,
              weeping over my grave.

She shows two tiny teeth
    in a sister-smile just for me.

          What am I doing? What have I done?

I need to get Esme settled

so I can think.

She likes a tune or two, so
I pick up my phone & scroll . . .

Before he went on the school trip,
Ravi sent me a playlist of
    his (so-called) classic tracks.

He called it, *Wish You Were Here* –
    but I never even bothered to
    open it.

I pop Esme onto a bean bag
& I click on the link for a listen.

Oh, Ravi.

Looks like he picked out
    all the cheesy best-mate songs
    from his dad's collection.

Every single song is about friendship.

Esme's still smiling, but tears are
    streaming down my face.

Carole King is singing
no matter what the season,
    I've got a friend.

Have I? Still?
Ravi, I need you now.
Will you still be there?

I listen to the song some more,
then blow my nose,
pick up the phone,
& call.

THE PLAN

Ravi scrapes his plate

& makes *yum-yum* faces
    at the giggling twins.

Although it's evening, the kitchen's very warm
& they're wearing nothing but nappies
    & chocolate ice cream.

Thanks, Mrs Andersen!
Ravi pushes his knife & fork
    together, super polite.

        I don't know how he could eat so much.
        My stomach is knotted with worry.
        Okay to go on the PlayStation?
        I ask Mum.

She nods,
    mellow with Prosecco.

Up in my room
    Ravi turns deadly serious.

He puts on music
    to cover our voices like we're spies,
sits on the edge of my bed &
    rubs his specs with my pillowcase.
You've got to get out of this.

        Tell me something I don't know.
        *Like – **how?***

Just give K1 back those drugs.

        It must be good to live in Ravi's world.
        So, what do I do?
        Just text him & say,
        'Hey, sorry, can't do it, bro'?

Why not? says Ravi.

I lift my shirt & show him
the peacock display that's
patterned over my ribs.
That's why not.

Ravi winces
& shuts up.

We listen in silence to Freddie Mercury
    belting it out
    about how he wants to
    break free . . .

Yeah, me too.
But it's all right for Freddie.
He's dead already.

Ravi cuts Freddie off

mid-yodel.

Panic flares behind the glint
    of my best friend's glasses.

I'm having a horrible thought, he says.
Why d'you think he told you not to open it?
It's not like you haven't seen drugs before . . .

We stare at each other.

We're both having the same

                    horrible

                        thought.

I don't need

to cut all the wrapping away.

The moment my scissors
   hit metal, we know.

K1 doesn't want me to
   take drugs
   across the enemy line

he wants me to
   take revenge.

Ravi's hard to convince

that telling our parents isn't the answer –
but I know they'd go straight to the feds.

Ravi still lives in a world
   where the good guys win:

I have to fill him in
   on what can happen to a snitch,
or – *& this is so much worse* –
to a snitch's family.

In the end,
   thank God,
he gets it.

It's late & Ravi has to go –

it's a school night, after all.

Don't worry, mate!
    he whispers on the doorstep,
as Mum fusses around
    with the rubbish.

I'll think of a plan!

That's good, because there's
    one thing I know for sure:

I can't give Fritz that gun.

If I do, someone will be dead
& it would be like
    I'd pulled the trigger myself.

I might be a crappy friend,
    a loser who doesn't deserve
    someone like Ravi –

but I'm not a murderer.

That night, I don't sleep.

I'm so restless
I'm almost rotating under my duvet
    at 33 rpm,
thinking about the gun
    wrapped in its black tape shroud
    three feet from my head.

Every time I start to drift to sleep
Ravi sends another link to
    stuff on *county lines*.

I know he means well
    but feeling stupid ain't helping.

At seven, Mum knocks to get
    me up for school,
    mug of tea in hand.

She's all about new starts this morning,
    as bubbly as Prosecco.

Today's a big day, she's not wrong.

For the twins,
    a couple of hours at nursery,
    settling in (like the curry).

For Mum,
    an hour or two at the office,
    onboarding (whatever that is).

For me,
    not much longer left
    living (if I'm unlucky).

Big day indeed.

Don't fall asleep again, champ!
Mum says, as she leaves my room & I say, don't worry, I'll be
down in a minute. I listen to her footsteps fade, then get up
& quietly open up the cupboard, *very* carefully
pull out a black-taped package the
size & shape of
a heavy book, and I wrap
it in a towel
then hide it
right at the
bottom of my
red sports bag.

Ravi agrees

the most important thing
    is keeping my family safe.

So he understands
    what it means
when at 7:16
    a text arrives:

GO PICK UP THE POST

On the doormat
    there's an envelope
with a train ticket
    tucked inside.

It *means* that K1
    knows exactly
    where I live,
& he wants me to know
    he knows.

I'll think of something,
    says Ravi.

And he does.

Mum's flattered
    that I want my family there
    to watch me race.

Really? she says,
    taping a new dressing on my cheek.
Are you sure?
The girls too?

All of you! I say.
I've got to keep
them out of the house,
out of harm's way.

If I can get away on time,
I'll pick them up & catch the bus
right over to the stadium.

Come anyway! I say,
hoping the desperation
doesn't show on my face.
Even if you're too late
to see me race.
I . . . just want you there.

She gives me a suspicious look
but then her mouth relaxes.
I'll do my best.

After breakfast

Ravi's knock is
    more of a soft *tap.*

When I open the door
his face is all question
???????????????

                    but I just nod my head –
                    the tiniest amount,

because Mum's eyes are fixed on my back
like a cat watching
    a sparrow.

297

Swinging my Adidas bag
over my shoulder,
I call back
over my shoulder,
Wish me luck then, Mum!

She has no idea
how much luck I'm going to need.

Mum made me promise
I'd do my very best today.

& I made her promise
she'd do her very best
to be there.

I've carried a lot

of things
on my back
but the weight
of the gun
that morning

is the weight of
guilt,

& I swear, man,
it's the heaviest
load to bear.

Ravi's humming 'Lean on Me'

on repeat, like that helps.

Well, it helps me*!*
    he says.

                                    I wish he'd shut up,
                                    cos I've got incoming.

From Mr R: *GOT YOUR SPORTS KIT?*

From K1: *GOT THE PACK?*

From Mr R: *MEET YOU AT 8:30 BY THE SCHOOL GATES*

From K1: *GO STRAIGHT TO THE STN. GET THE 8:30*

                    My thumb's jumping between the bubbles –
                            how can I be in two places
                                    at the same time?

Mr R: *I'LL BE WATCHING OUT FOR YOU.*
        DON'T BE LATE.

K1: *WE'RE WATCHING U. DON'T MISS IT.*

We're near the entrance to the school now:
    kids are trickling towards it
    like asteroids to a black hole.

                            My hand hovers over the screen.

In the early sun, in the distance,
    the station roof glows copper.

Soon the babies will be safe at nursery
    & Mum on her way to work.

I look at Ravi. He nods.

We're at the school gates.

Keep calm, my friend –
 says Ravi.
It's time to commence Plan A.

He's making out he's chill,
but I know he's really worried, cos
 his glasses are steaming up.

You go to the station.
Do what we said.
I'll stall Mr R.

He gives me a quick,
 embarrassed hug that makes
 a group of passing Year 7s
 explode into giggles.

I'll call you. Stay on the line.
Ravi removes the misted glasses & smiles.
We got this.

He looks at his watch as
 the registration bell goes off
 like an air-raid siren.
Children run for cover all around.

But you better get going.

I've got to make the 8:30.

I start to jog towards the station,
    the weight of the gun
    bumping against my back
    dangerously.

Too late, I think:
Is it loaded?
It can't be loaded, can it?
Or if it is
    there'll be a safety catch
    or something.

Sweat trickles
    down between
    my shoulder blades.

Ravi rings &
    whispers in my ear –
It's going to be okay.
Just keep going.
Just keep going.

I have to believe
    it'll work because
    there is no Plan B.

Crossing the road by the mall,
    I look left-right.

Who's watching?
Who's watching?
Where are they?

Into the wide sweep

of the station car park, I run.

I'm bobbing & weaving through
the mad commuter rush.

I'm jogging on the spot under
the display board that says
`08:27`

I'm scanning across the line
of blinking letters –
Where's my train?

Ravi's voice in my ear,
It's Platform 6, relax! It's always Platform 6.

Actually, for Ravi's plan to work
it's *gotta* be Platform 6,
the one with the sneaky side exit.

On Platform 6
the 08:30 has already
huffed open its doors.

A parade of passengers
are pushing against my back –

Don't touch me!

I'm dodging clear,
out of the stream,
standing to the side of the barrier,
fishing through my pockets for the ticket.

Glancing back at the entrance
I lock eyes with –

N
 a
  t
   h
    a
     n

slouching up against a wall,
picking his teeth.

Slowly he raises two fingers
& aims them
        straight at
            my heart.

The sweat across my
    forehead freezes.

Ravi!
I mutter,
turning my head
away from Nathan's gaze.
Nathan's here. He's watching me.

Ravi's voice is urgent:
*Can he see the side exit
    from where he is?*

No – he's by the entrance.
The train's blocking it.

*Okay, that's good.
Get on the train.*

. . .
Okay, I'm on.

Wave at Nathan.

What?

Wave!

A cleaner steps though from the driver's cab
    clutching a sack of rubbish.
He gives me a funny look.

I fake a smile
& wave at Nathan –

who gives me the finger.

Okay, now he's seen you're on,
move up
    through the train
    to the carriage by the side exit.
Can he still see you?

                                   I can't see him,
                                   so I guess not.

Good.

The guard blows his whistle.

                                        I count:
One . . . two . . . three . . . four . . . five –

Ravi shouts
NOW! –

I jump out onto the platform

a nanosecond before the doors hiss shut

& hurdle over the side gate,

my heart a racing engine
that only slows down

when the train has left the station
without me.

    .
    .
    .
    .
    .
    .
    .
    .
    .
    .
    .
    .

I reckon
I've got half an hour
    before the train arrives
& Fritz finds out
    I'm not on it.

RUNNING

Ravi's voice

cuts though my panting.
Are you out?

Yeah!

Good.
Mr R keeps asking where you are . . .
I keep making up excuses.

Ravi & Betty
     volunteered to marshal
& make up some story why I'm late,
     delay the bus.

Keep stalling.
I'm coming!

Hurry! Now to ditch the –
     he lowers his voice –
     thing.
GO!

Then
     Ravi's internal jukebox
     drops another disc –

& I swear
if I get through this alive,
next time he plays
'Take Me to the River'
I'm going to
drop that bloody vinyl
in the water.

The River Wendel

loops around the city
    like a circling hand,

moving a tide of scum from the
    east-side estates
    to the posh houses in the west.

Up the road from the station,
    where trees dip in to cool their leaves,
    & a few weeks –
    a lifetime – ago,
    I delivered to Jordan Ikes's mother,
    now I stand on the bank, ribs heaving,
    delivering a package
    from my sports bag.

Anyone watching?   *arc through the air –*
    No.
I lob it, watching it

a distress flare
    that drops
    with a *splosh* in the water,
    & sinks, extinguished.

Forever, I hope.

I take a careful photo
    & add a digital
X marks the spot.

I've gotta go like an express train

to get to the Districts
& make my mother proud.

                                    I don't count strides.
                                      Instead I chant,
                                        I can do this
                                        I can do this
                                    over & over & over.

Ravi calls me
    when I'm still
    huffing up the hill by the mall.

Mr R's not happy!
Ravi's voice is a whisper.
He says he won't wait much longer.
You've got five minutes,
    that's all.

                                    Now there's no option:
                                    I have to run through
                                        the shortcut.
                                        The alleyway.
                                        The death trap.

Good luck!
Ravi rings off.

My lungs are snatching at the air,

legs burning
    on the lead-up to the alleyway,

& I won't lie,
I'm totally *bricking* it.

                    I can – do this. I can – do this.
                    I can – do this. I can – do this.

The sun & my sweat
    are blurring my vision:

I swipe my T-shirt across my face & blink
    the entrance to the alley into focus

                  I can – do this. I can – do –

There's a dark car
    at the corner by the old stone arch.

As I pass,
the window rolls down
& a man's voice shouts,
ERIK! ERIK! STOP!

            My heart goes into instant
                f$_{i}$b^{r}il^{l}at^{i}on.
                Can I escape?
            Only if I throw myself
        under the wheels of the
           rush-hour traffic.

The car door opens.

A tall, dark, figure
    unfolds himself from the driver's seat
& steps into my path.

I've never been so glad

to see him in my life.

It's Mr Choudhri – *Mr Choudhri!* –
    who stands there,
impeccably dressed
    as always
    in a charcoal three-piece suit.

He looks slightly puzzled.
Ravi called. Said to meet you here.
There's an emergency?
– Something about a race?
I can give you a lift
    if you like.

                    I could have kissed him
                    or cried with relief
                    but instead I just pant,
                    Um, yeah, thanks!
                    & get in, quick.

Mr Choudhri

keeps up a gentle conversation,
    a river of verbal muzak
        for the twenty-minute ride.

I have no idea
    what he's on about;
something about the Greeks
& the first Olympic Games.

I know he knows
I'm not really listening.

I keep my mouth shut
& close my eyelids too:

I don't want to talk.
I don't want to think.

Any time round about now,
that train's going to hit the buffers.

YOU'RE LATE, ANDERSEN!

We pull in at the stadium just
    behind the minibus.

YOU'RE OFF THE TEAM!
Mr Robinson yells as he
    gets off,
tapping his watch
    like a compass.

                          I feel sick.
                  After all this effort?
                       Sorry, sir.

I'm calling your
    mother to get you! This –

Mr Choudhri coughs softly.
He walks around the car &
    holds out his hand.

Mr Robinson? I am Ravi's father.
I don't believe we've met.

313

My apologies for Erik's tardiness.
Entirely my fault.

His slim hand disappears
    into Mr R's giant paw &
    I think he must've pressed a valve or something
because Mr R deflates
    like a football.

Really?
Oh. Oh . . . all right then.
Erik, go & get changed.

Mr R looks at me properly
    then does a double-take.
What the hell did you do to your face?

The changing room

fills up quickly.

I cross the room to get some water &
jeers *bounce over the partitions*

like squash balls.

What happened to you, Andersen?
Mr Nelson get his own back?

                My heart sinks.
              I don't believe it.
              Ben & Travis?!
                    Here?

They must be on punishment,
    conscripted into the marshalling
    chain gang,
setting cones in
not-so-straight lines.

                              This is a disaster!
                    Why didn't Ravi warn me?

Walking in,
Ravi meets my glare with a
    helpless shrug.

Ben pulls out his phone –

                              & I know I'm dead –

but Mr Robinson intercepts it
like the rugby pro he is.

Thank you, Mr Pagua. I'll take that.
No phones, remember?

He pats his pocket.
    I already have young Mr Choudhri's, but
    there's room for more.
Yours too, Travis.

Travis scowls, but gives.
Mr Robinson's tracksuit pockets are bulging
as he strides from the room.

                              I sink onto a bench.

Ravi sinks down beside me & whispers
    Sorry I couldn't warn you! He took –

                              Don't worry. I get it.
                    Thanks for the lift from your dad.
                    I close my eyes. I'm safe for now.

When I open them again
Mr Robinson's holding out an ice pack
& a can of Coke.

THESE'LL FIX ANYTHING!
    he says
    at subwoofer volume.

                              If I didn't know better,
                              I'd think he'd gone soft.

There's quite a crowd

come to watch
    us *elite athletes*
    do our stuff.

We funnel out, blinking
    into the sun & a sea
    of clapping & cheering.

Are they here?
When I shade my eyes & squint
    along the line,
I find a tiny wavelet
    just for me – <u>*YES!*</u>

Alice & Esme & Mum
    safe in the stands,
Mum standing &
    yelling, *Go, Erik!*

Yeah.
Go, me.

On your marks . . .

Get set . . . GO!

Four hundred metres
   goes by pretty fast.

                    I'm birthing
               a new Erik Andersen,

I'm feeling pain,

                    an Erik who
           thinks before he acts.

fighting for breath,

           I know I can't change
                  what's past,

telling myself not to
look over my shoulder

             but from here on
              I can be better –

as I stretch out my stride,
& my heart's almost bursting,

           I can be who my dad
              believed I was.

only thirty . . . twenty . . .
ten metres to go . . .

        I can make my mother proud.

I'm crossing the line.

You didn't seriously

think I'd get gold?

I've just been beaten up,
scared to death,
& sprinted halfway
    across the town –
get real.

I did come *fourth* though –
with a personal best.
I'd call that winning.

No medal but a
    pat on the back from Mr R
    that lands on my ribs
    like a hammer throw.

No medal but a
Mum who holds me tightly.
    That's amazing, Erik!
    I had no idea that
    you could run like that!

I hate it that
I'm going to have to
burst her bubble.

Oh, Mum.
There's so much you don't know
about me & running.

So much
you're about to find out.

Well done, Erik!

says Betty, looking me in the eye for once.

Cheers!
Ravi . . . I grab his arm. A word?

I draw him away from the group.
Ravi's dad stayed to watch the race;
he's chatting to Betty & my mum.

I show Ravi my phone,
the messages that just flooded in.

Ah. K1 got the news, then.
Ravi rubs his glasses.
Reads some more of the
    furious tsunami.
Wow. Time for the rest of the plan?

Can we all go back to yours?
Will your dad mind?
We're not safe at mine.

Ravi looks at his dad.
No problem. Just do what you gotta do.
Be quick.

My best friend hands me a pen & paper
along with a nugget of know-how:
Apparently, a gun can still yield prints
    years after being submerged.

Who knew?

Crouched in a toilet cubicle,

I'm writing my very last message
        to K1:

      To K1
      No more.
      I'm out.

   I'm shaking. It's hard to write.

      The piece'll have your prints.
      It's in a safe place
      along with the SIM cards.

          I chew the end of Ravi's pen.
          He hates that.

             I won't snitch, I promise.
             The feds won't get them
             as long as we stay safe.
             LEAVE US ALONE.

                I'm so bold,
                so brave . . .

        I can feel my terror sliding in a tide,
               chill as gunmetal
               through my blood.

I don't want anything from K1

Nothing more to tie us.

I thumbnail out
    the precious metal
    of the SIMs,
worth so much more
      than their weight in gold.

After a second's thought,
I slip the slivers underneath the
      sticking plaster on my cheek.

Ravi's not the only one
    with smarts.

The note gets wrapped

around the phones,
the phones dropped in
    my sweaty sock.

Travis & Ben are still out
    on the track, picking up cones.

Ben's bag is tucked under the bench.
A waft of weed comes from it.
I zip open its mouth just wide enough
    to add the stink of my sock –

then leg it.

Mrs Choudhri's dining table

is covered with a plastic cloth.
She says the swirling pattern
     tells a tale:
a battle between good & evil.

> There's not much good in my story.
> I trace the curls with my finger,
> filling my mother in
> on the evil truth.

Ravi's printed out some information that
     he said would help my mum to understand,
but what she reads on county lines
     turns her face pale as paper.

She puts the pages down
     with shaking hands.
Quietly. Too quietly.

> *Say something, Mum.*

> I wish she would shout –
> But she can't even look at me.

Finally, she speaks,
in a voice bled white.

What have you done, Erik?
Oh my God –
     whatever
     have
     you
     done?

But why?

She keeps asking,
    & every time she does,
her shoulders sag a little lower,
the lines across her face
    look more like
    knife wounds.

What did I do? she asks.
Was it my fault?

        I want to shout, *YES!*
        I want to roar it loud enough
        to make the walls rock
        with my guilt & rage –
        Yes! Yes! It was you!

        But it wasn't her,
        or it wasn't *only* her.

        I know I've gotta
        own this for myself, but
        it's so much effort
        to trace it back,
        & right now
        I'm just too tired,
        & so I say
        Yes. No.
        I don't know.

        Sorry.
        Sorry.
        Sorry.

We hole up

in Ravi's spare room
    for days.
We're hiding,
waiting for the storm to blow
    over our heads.

We watch a lot of TV to pass the time.
Sometimes we perform our own screenplays,
every argument a different genre:

<u>THRILLER</u>

MOTHER
We've got to go to the police.

SON
You crazy? K1 would kill me. Or you.
Or the babies. Or all of us.

MOTHER
You're exaggerating.

SON
You feelin' lucky, punk?

<u>SIT-COM</u>

MOTHER
You had a gun! In our house!

SON
I'm sorry, Mum. I thought it was
just . . . you know . . . drugs.

MOTHER
(rolls her eyes)
Just . . . you know . . . drugs.

<u>DOCUDRAMA</u>

                    MOTHER
        I've got to involve the school.

                    SON
        You do that, they'll throw me out.

                    MOTHER
            They can't do that.

                    SON
        You watch them. I'll be out of there
        so fast! Then I'll have to go to the
        PRU & the PRU's full of kids who
                work for K1.

                    MOTHER
                Seriously?

                    SON
                Believe it.

<u>CRINGE COMEDY</u>

                    MOTHER
        You delivered cocaine to Jordan
                Ikes's mother?

                    SON
        If it helps, I don't think she
                recognised me.

                    MOTHER
        She's Head of the PTA! Wait till
            I tell the girls—

                    SON
                    MUM!

            (canned laughter)

                    325

MOTHER
I can't believe I was so blind!

SON
Honestly? Neither can I.

MOTHER
(slaps him)

But we keep coming back to . . .

TRAGEDY

MOTHER
So basically, we're sitting here like
ducks, hoping K1 feels too chicken to
make a move?

SON
I guess . . . yeah.

MOTHER
Jesus, Erik.
(Starts crying again.)

You can't live like that.

Nobody can.
Nobody should have to.

I see my mother
    not feeling *safe*,
never turning her back on the twins
    in the park,
not even for a second.

We talk
    & talk
        & talk
            it through.

Round & round & round
until we reach a dead end,
            a cul-de-sac
            of decision.

Mum's going to apply for a transfer.
We're moving.

Goodbye

to the house where I was born,
the creaking boards to dodge,
the door frame's tidemark height chart,
the football scuffmarks on the
    brick wall outside –
Goodbye to my childhood.

Goodbye
    to the only city I've ever known,
the back-alley shortcuts, the
    bus routes & their crabby drivers,
the estates, corner shops & mall,
& of course, to the Flo.

Goodbye
    to my school,
closed now for summer
(disabled but not disarmed),
& to Mr R, who nods like he understands
    so much more than I say.

Goodbye
   to my best friend, Ravi,
my only real friend,
& to his family, who
   have sheltered & helped us
& driven me nearly insane
   with their taste in music.

& finally

Goodbye
   to Dad, in his corner
   of the churchyard.

Yesterday, we all went to plant
   a butterfly bush on his grave.

Grows like crazy,
   thrives on neglect,
   attracts pollinators,
reads Ravi, from the tag.

Sounds like teenage boys,
   says Mum.

She & I stay behind for a while.

By Dad's grave

Mum says *sorry* to me for the bits
   that are on her,
(but maybe weren't exactly her fault).

She says sorry for Jonny too –
though not for the twins; we will
   never be sorry about my sisters.

She says I need to let myself grieve.

I've kept my sadness shut away
   like savings in a biscuit tin,
     in a box I labelled *Dad*.

I haven't let myself cry for him:
only the rage escapes from time to time, like
   stuffing leaking out the seams.

Mum says it's okay to be angry with Dad
   for dying, even if he didn't mean to.

She says I can blame Dad for the red hair too.

She says I can tell Dad how I feel,
   however I feel.
He can take it.

Then she leaves us alone.

I look up some words of Norwegian.

Jeg savner deg.
(I miss you)

Jeg er lei meg.
(I'm sorry)

Takk for alt!
(Thanks for everything)

I tell Dad what's happened
   since he left,
& then I listen . . .

maybe not listen, exactly,
   but *imagine* what
   he would have said.

Afterwards, I get up
& touch his name,
   carved so deep.

Andrea
Johann
Anders

Beloved
husband
father

Born 31.05.1
Died 31.03.2

Ha det, pappa.
(Goodbye, Dad.)

CROSSING
THE LINE

At a crazy time of night

under a full summer moon,
everything we own gets loaded
    into a huge, hired van.

A friend of Ravi's dad
    takes the wheel.

Behind it,
stashed like a secret
    into the Choudhris'
    battered black car,

the Andersen family

                    crosses

                                    the county line.

THE END

                    (Except it isn't.)

ROLL THE CREDITS

Stay in your seat!

There's time to finish the popcorn.
We've got the updates to come,
the cheesy bio-pic, *where are they now?*
    wrap-up cameos.

So . . . *Click!*
Picture this.

It's a year on
    from when Mum & I
    moved house.

We'll all step up
    to take our bows,
    in no particular order.

ME
I don't bow, but I
    raise my arm in an air-punch
because the new *me*
    is a boxer, a proper fighter,
lean & hard & healthy.

Mr R knew someone
who knew someone
who had a gym for boys like me.

                                    RAVI
                       is still my best mate,
       still the biggest nerd in the world,
            still head deep into books,
               still torturing the world
             with his taste in music.

Not still jogging though:
he's dropped it for dancing
(in the ballroom style) with Betty,
who has nearly, *almost,*
forgiven me.

CHANTELLE
took over the
    till of the trainer shop.
Ravi says she taps at the buttons
    with glossy claws long as a *Therizinosaurus,*
& stares through the screen of
    her bright blonde hair
    with a glassy gaze.

BEN & TRAVIS
weren't invited back
for sixth form – not a shocker.
Ravi says you can find them feeding the cats,
loitering in the long grey shadows
of the Flo, looking more & more
mangy themselves.

MY MUM
is a survivor
    who thinks I'm a survivor too,
but she doesn't realise
    we're still in danger.
I know I should tell her –
but I just can't bear
    to break her
    all over again, because –

& you already know this, don't you? –

it's still not actually

THE END

I thought it was over.

I thought I was free.
Until one day, without warning –

Fritz appears in my house
his dark-jowled scowl
    staring grainily up at me
    from my doormat.

Drug Lord Stabbed to Death in Gangland War

My fear trembles
    that screaming headline
    to a blur.
The police are hunting for a child –
They don't say who,
but I think I can guess.

They just want to talk to him.
Maybe he was simply
    in the wrong place
    at the wrong time?

No shit.
Of course he was.

We all are.

I fold the paper

& push it to the
    bottom of the recycling.

If I'm lucky,
Mum won't ever
    find out.

Mum says

I look *peaky*.
Peaky?

I'm pale, apparently.

                                                I feel *sick*.

She says I gotta
    take my sisters shopping,
    get some air.

I can't say no, but
    I can't say why not,
so Trygg comes too,
    my canine comfort blanket.

Wherever I go these days,

Trygg follows,
padding softly behind me,
toenails click-click-clicking
    on our wooden floors.

My bed smells very doggy,
but that's better than
    the smell of bud.

My father used to
    have a dog called Trygg
    when he was a boy.
The name means *safe*.

We got this Trygg from the dogs' home.
She'd been looking for a
    family for months,
but she's a Staffie:
got a bad rep.

Truth is, my gentle Tryggie
    wouldn't hurt a fly –
though that's a secret
    she & I are keeping to ourselves.

Now, she pads along beside the buggy,
nose to my thigh
    as always.

The high street's heaving with shoppers.
Good. I feel safer in crowds.
Not safe.
Saf*er*.

The twins' favourite shop

survived the pandemic,
    unfortunately.

I buckle under pressure
& agree
    we can poke at some teddies.

Inside, they build bears
    but they don't like dogs, so
    Trygg gets time out,
tied to the buggy that's
    tied to the bike rack.

She's not happy.
Her tail curls tightly
    through her stubby legs.

Whimpering softly, she
    pulls at the leash &
    I tie another knot
    to hold her
    fast.

Five minutes, Trygg, tops!
I kiss her sweet muzzle
& get a lungful
of doggie breath back.

She whines like she'll
    never see us again.

Dogs!
I say to my sisters.
No faith, eh?

Alice & Esme flap
    their podgy fingers in goodbye.

It's hot & crowded in there

So much bear fur flying
    I can barely breathe, but
    Alice & Esme are having
    the time of their tiny lives.

It's ten minutes
    before I can pull them out, &
Esme's yelling *NoNoNONONO!*
    so loud that at first I don't hear

the woman by the bike rack,
screaming.

The girls

are like anchors
    dragging on my arms as
    I struggle forward –

                    Shut UP, Esme!

to the small crowd
    gathering round the woman
    standing by the bike racks –

                    Come on, Alice, PLEASE!

who's got her
    hands pressed to her face –

                    What is it, what's the matter?

staring down at –

                    My dog! That's my dog!

the dung-coloured shape
    lying on the ground,
    completely
    totally
    still.

The next moments

cannon into each other
    like dominoes *toppling*.

Screaming lady screams,
I just saw the dog just lying there!
like she thinks
    I'd think
        she did it.

Helpful arms scoop the
    shrieking twins into their buggy.

Helpful voices shout,
There's a vet's just over there!
You grab the dog, lad, I'll push the buggy!

Grunting with the strain,
I bend my knees &
    hoist Trygg's sack-of-potatoes,
    ridiculously heavy,
    dead-weight body
    into my arms, expecting
    as I lift her, to see
    a spreading scarlet stain beneath –
but there's nothing.

Then I *run*.

The vet is

tall & angular, white-coated.

He says,
It's okay, son, I've got her,
& lifts the lolling Tryggie from my arms.

I wait for ages outside the
closed door of the consulting room.
There are murmurs inside,
the beep of a monitor.

I'm rocking my sleeping sisters.
The buggy's like a jiggling foot,
^{up}-$_{down}$-^{up}-$_{down}$-^{up}-$_{down}$.

When the vet comes out,
his face has lost its kindness.
She'll live. You're lucky.

Relief floods my mouth with spit.
I think I might be sick.
I can smell my sweat:
it's stinking out the room.

It was ketamine, most likely –

What?

He looks at me, frowning a furrow
in a face that's mostly forehead –
I suppose you'd call it K, young man.

There's a horrible pause.
. . . . . .

342

I knew it.

I knew this wouldn't be the end.

Did you poison this dog?

NO! Of course not!
I yelp.

Well, someone did.
This was tucked into her collar.

He hands me a
scrunched up ten-pound note with
red sharpie scrawled all the way
across Queen Elizabeth's smirk.

GIVE ME THE SIM CARDS
OR
YOUR SISTERS ARE NEXT.

& all at once . . .

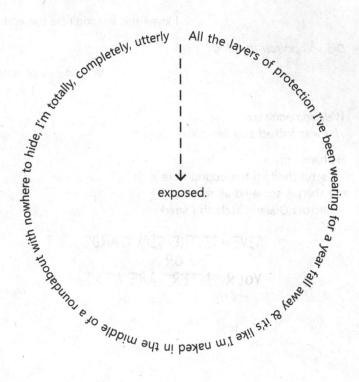

All the layers of protection I've been wearing for a year fall away & it's like I'm naked in the middle of a roundabout with nowhere to hide, I'm totally, completely, utterly

exposed.

I call Ravi.

You've got to get help, he says,
the Beatles playing softly
     in the background.

*There are other places you can go,
     you know. Not just the feds.*

*There are people who can help –
who understand about stuff like this . . .*

They're on your side. No judgement.

He tosses me a link
     which lands in my phone
     like a lifebelt.

*Check them out.
Seriously, Erik, do it.
They help kids who
     get caught up like this.
Kids like you.*

Please. PLEASE. Just call them.

                    & because he sounds close to tears,
                         & because my friend Ravi
                         is usually right – at least
                         about everything but music –

                                             I do.

My hands are shaking

so much I can hardly
stab at
the screen.

You answer, *Hello!*
like you were expecting
    my call.

Your voice is warm.

Before we start, you say
you need to ask me something.

It's such a simple question,
but only someone
    who *gets it*
    would ask.

You say,
Do you feel safe?

                                                             & I find myself
telling you

everything.

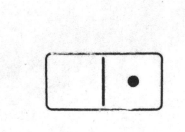

The Soundtrack

Ravi says that I should share the tunes he shared with me.
He says they're retro chic. I say listen at your peril.

Seriously, don't blame me if your ears fall off.

'Baby Don't Cry' by INXS
'Summer Holiday' by Cliff Richard and the Shadows
'The Eton Rifles' by the Jam
'Rubber Bullets' by 10cc
'I Shot the Sheriff' by Bob Marley & the Wailers
'Can't Help Falling in Love' by Elvis Presley
'(I Can't Get No) Satisfaction' by the Rolling Stones
'Rocket Man' by Elton John
'Don't Stop Me Now' by Queen
'Sorry Seems to Be the Hardest Word' by Elton John
'Hello' by Adele
'Sailing' by Rod Stewart
'Stayin' Alive' by the Bee Gees
'The Sound of Silence' by Simon & Garfunkel
'I Want to Break Free' by Queen
'Take Me to the River' by Talking Heads
'Help!' by the Beatles
& *every single track* by Elvis Costello, no lie.

And these are the tracks on his 'Wish You Were Here' playlist:

'You've Got a Friend' by Carole King
'Wish You Were Here' by Pink Floyd
'You're My Best Friend' by Queen
'You've Got a Friend in Me' by Randy Newman
'Lean on Me' by Bill Withers
'Stand by Me' by Ben E. King
'Friends' by Flight of the Conchords

The Children's Society

We believe every child should have a safe, happy childhood. But we know things aren't always that simple. Across the country, lots of young people are struggling with big life challenges, and The Children's Society is here for them when they need help.

For example, we support young people who have been or are at risk of being exploited. This is when a young person is forced into criminal or sexual activities. Criminals might groom young people in their community or online by giving them things like gifts, drugs, money or gaming credits. But they then demand 'favours' in return and may force children to do things that are illegal or dangerous like carrying drugs in county lines operations.

Young people have the right to feel safe, wherever they are. If you're ever sent anywhere or asked to do anything that makes you feel unsafe, unsure or uncomfortable, there is help out there. It's important to remember that if you're being exploited or someone is trying to exploit you, you are not to blame and you deserve support. Tell an adult you trust or report it.

There are lots of people and organisations that can help you, like The Children's Society. We work with the police, social care, businesses, and staff working in public spaces like shopping centres and train stations to make sure they're looking out for children and can spot the signs of exploitation. And our support workers help young people rebuild their lives and stay safe.

Getting Help

If you or a young person you know is in immediate danger, call 999. If it's not an emergency, call 101 to speak to the police or report your concerns online at www.police.uk/pu/contact-the-police/report-a-crime-incident. Calls to 999 and 101 are free to make. You can also contact your local social care department, via www.gov.uk/report-child-abuse.

If you – or anyone you know – has been affected by issues in this book, below are some UK organisations you could turn to.

The Children's Society supports children and young people at risk of exploitation, and who are being exploited, helping to protect them and then rebuild their lives. The national charity advocates for children to be treated as victims, not criminals, and for their voices to be heard. It works alongside the police, local authorities, the NHS, schools and other organisations to help them identify exploitation and improve their responses to children and young people.
www.childrenssociety.org.uk

The Metropolitan Police have information about signs to look out for that may indicate someone is involved in county lines, with further links to support agencies: www.met.police.uk/advice/advice-and-information/cl/county-lines

The National Crime Agency county lines page explains more about county lines and indicators of exploitation in your area, with further links to support agencies: www.nationalcrimeagency.gov.uk/what-we-do/crime-threats/drug-trafficking/county-lines

ChildLine is a confidential service for children and young people up to age 19, giving them access to a Childline counsellor about any problem causing them harm or concern. This can be over the phone, 1-2-1 online chat or by setting up an email locker (inc. BSL & other languages). Website provides a range of games, videos and resources for additional support.

Call: 0800 1111 (free)

www.childline.org.uk

Family Action provides practical, emotional and financial support to those who are experiencing poverty, disadvantage and social isolation through around 120 community-based services. Its **Familyline** service provides free support for parents and adult family members.

Call: 0808 802 6666 (free) (Monday–Friday, 9am–9pm)

Text: 07537 404 282

Email: familyline@family-action.org.uk

www.family-action.org.uk (live chat)

Out of hours, text FAMILYACTION to 85258

www.safe4me.co.uk/support-services has details about support services nationally for young people impacted by child criminal and sexual exploitation. They also have lots of information regarding specific forms of exploitation, understanding trauma, rights and the law and much more.

Runaway Helpline, part of the UK charity Missing People, is a free confidential support service for young people aged 11–17 thinking about running away, who have already run away, or have been away and returned – also for others worried someone else is going to run away, being treated badly or abused. Trained professionals are accessible to young people 24/7 to support them with issues causing them concern or harm.

Call: 116 000 (free) (9am–11pm every day)
Text: 116 000 (free)
Email: 116000@www.runawayhelpline.org.uk
www.runawayhelpline.org.uk for
1-2-1 online chat: (2.30–9.30pm every day)

Winston's Wish, a childhood bereavement charity, offers a wide range of practical support and guidance to bereaved children, their families and professionals. For advice and guidance on supporting a bereaved child or young person, contact the Helpline team on 08088 020 021 (free, Monday–Friday, 8am–8pm), or email ask@winstonswish.org.

Author's Note

In 2019, my friend's fourteen-year-old son – who'd been bullied and was disruptive at school – became aggressive. He was staying out all night, smoking weed. At first, his parents put it down to 'teenage', but by the end of that year he was so ill with anxiety, he'd stopped eating; he was so scared, he couldn't even walk across town.

What was he so scared of? Eventually he confessed. *Gangs.* He'd been running drugs and weapons for a gang, and now he wasn't safe anywhere. They were even threatening his family: it felt like there was no escape.

That was the first I'd ever heard of 'county lines' child exploitation. County *what?* I hunted around for information, but most of what I found was buried in police reports and documentaries. Although authorities already suspected there were *tens of thousands* of children in England being exploited by gangs to run and sell drugs, these children's experiences weren't reflected in books, or films, or on TV.

That's why I wanted to write about it: to spread the word about this destruction of so many young lives. Lockdown made it much worse: today county lines is an epidemic among Britain's vulnerable young people. If it's happening to you or to a friend, I want you to know you aren't alone, you aren't to blame, and you can reach out for help.

My friend's son is now, thankfully, safe, and he's piecing his future together. He wants to help others if he can, and we talked for hours while he answered my many questions. I've used my imagination, of course: Erik's story, as I have written it, is fiction. But many of the details of my character's recruitment (grooming) and his life selling drugs in a regional city are real and came from our conversations. Because I was writing outside my own experience, it was my responsibility to do a lot of research: I read reports, the little fiction I could find, and listened to youth workers, to other young people and to families of county lines victims.

I'm very grateful that The Children's Society gave their time to talk to me and read *Crossing the Line* for authenticity. They know that children caught up in county lines are victims, not criminals, and they work to get them vital support and protection.

If you recognise yourself, or anyone you know, in Erik's story, then please don't feel you have to cope with this on your own. I can't promise a magic wand – I wish I could – but I hope very much that you will find someone, perhaps in the previous pages, who will listen to you and help you.

Acknowledgements

I always thought that saying 'thank you' would be so easy, after the hard work of actually writing a book. But in the end, so many people helped me with *Crossing the Line*, I'm scared I'll leave someone out. Or else, make some mad Oscar-acceptance speech that just goes on and on and on and on and on and – See what I mean? But I have to start somewhere. So here's a massive shout-out to:

The *real* Erik and his family, without whom there would be no book and I would never have understood that county lines isn't just a thing that happens to 'other people'. Thank you for your courage in talking to me.

Tesfa and The Children's Society, for advising me, reading and approving my manuscript, and for all the amazing work you do with and on behalf of young people. I'm glad Ravi could tell Erik that help was out there.

The other readers who were kind enough to tell me where I got it right or wrong: Jane (mother of a county lines victim), 'Erik', Joe and Hetty. Thanks also to Ananjan, who told this particular couch potato what it feels like to run.

Henry Blake, former children's worker and the maker of the bleakly brilliant film *County Lines*, for taking the time to talk to me and share your experience.

Maddy, who booted me up the arse to be a writer in the first place. I owe you.

Tim and the rest of London Bridge Writers Group, who saw *Crossing the Line* in its infancy on lockdown screens, gave me feedback as I wrote a very hurried first draft and have cheered me on ever since.

The students and staff on the MA in Writing for Young People at Bath Spa, for the reassurance, hand-holding and encouragement; especially those who chipped in with ideas for discussions points, my tutor Finbar Hawkins and the 'Lovely Lift Ladies' for egging me on to f₀rmaᵗtᵢNᵍ madness.

Genius verse novelists like Sarah Crossan, Jason Reynolds, Kwame Alexander, Elizabeth Acevedo, Lucy Cuthew, Dean Atta, Louisa Reid and Manjeet Mann, who have inspired and astonished me and pushed the boundaries of what is possible in this form.

My agent Eve White and your team, for your faith in me, your perseverance, guidance and formidable negotiation skills!

Andrew Bannecker, for a cover design that makes me stop what I'm doing and stare open-mouthed, because you've captured Erik and his dilemma in such an endearing way.

My editor Emma Matthewson and the rest of the brilliant team at Hot Key, especially Talya, Tia (the other one), Sasha, Graeme, Dom, Emma and Amber. You understood so perfectly what I was trying to do and helped me to do it. Thank you so much for making my dream come true.

And finally, the biggest *thank you* of all to my family: my children, who have reluctantly adjudicated on the choice of so many words, and my husband Simon, who is my rock, my provider of calm, of meals on the table and (unwittingly) Ravi's playlist. Thank you for being the background music of my life.

Points for Discussion

Here are some ideas for you to think about or discuss when you have finished reading *Crossing the Line*.

1. The book starts with Erik asking, 'Do you feel *safe*?' How did this affect you? Who did you think Erik was telling his story to at the start, and did that change at the end?

2. Erik says, 'Seems like bad decisions / stack like dominoes. / When one topples, they all go.' Have you ever made one wrong decision that seemed to set off a whole load of others? How could you have stopped your dominoes from tumbling?

3. When Erik meets K1 and is on the edge of making the choice that will affect everything that follows, he explains it was 'all those other dominoes leaning on my back'. How far do you agree that the weight of other pressures pushed him into agreeing?

4. 'It wasn't a choice, not really.' Do you agree that Erik had no choice about whether to 'go country'? What would you have done if you were Erik? What risks was Erik taking by carrying the gun?

5. At one point Erik refers to the others in the trap house as his 'fam'. Why do you think he craves this feeling of belonging? How does his experience at the seaside change his view of gangs? Who in the book really functions as Erik's family?

6. What is your reaction to Erik's mum? What choices did *she* make which affected everything that followed? Do you feel that

359

she could have helped her son more, or did you sympathise with her? Or both?

7. What do you think of Ravi's attempts to try to stop Erik? If you had a friend you thought was caught up with county lines, how could you try to help them?

8. What was your response to K1 and the members of the county lines gangs? Do you think they seem realistic? What factors do you think make Erik vulnerable to gang leaders like K1?

9. How realistic is the depiction of school? What makes it seem authentic or inauthentic to you? What do you think the school should have done to help Erik? Could it have prevented him becoming caught up in county lines?

10. Do you think the ending is realistic? What do you think happens to Erik and his family after the book finishes? Can you think of any alternative endings, and what would they add to the story?

11. The novel is written in verse. How does that change your expectations? Does it make it more accessible to you, or more challenging? Has this book altered your view of what is – and what is not – poetry?

12. What do you think of the way the words are set out on the page – the use of different fonts and concrete poetry? How does it affect the way you take in the information?

13. What different formats or media can you find in the book (for example text messages)? What do you think about mixing up different formats? What is the effect of the author not using conventional poem titles?

14. And finally . . . what did you learn from reading *Crossing the Line*? Who will you recommend it to? Do you think this is an important book for young people to read?

Please refer to 'Getting Help' on page 352 if you or anyone you know is affected by county lines.

About the Author

Crossing the Line is Tia Fisher's debut novel. In her spare time, she works in a children's library and is also completing an MA in Writing for Young People at Bath Spa University. She has published poems in *The Rialto* and been longlisted for the Mslexia Children's Novel Award. Tia lives in South London with her husband and two teenage children (who wish she'd stop mining them for source material).

Thank you for choosing a Hot Key book!

For all the latest bookish news, freebies and exclusive

content, sign up to the Hot Key newsletter – scan the

QR code or visit lnk.to/HotKeyBooks

Follow us on social media:

bonnierbooks.co.uk/HotKeyBooks